S0-AZD-343

3 2109 00357 6668

WITHDRAWN
University Libraries
University of Memphis

WITHDRAWN
University Libraries
University of Memphis

Wilderness Journey

by the same author

THE BUFFALO KNIFE

Illustrated by Paul Galdone

Wilderness Journey

WILLIAM O. STEELE

New York
Harcourt, Brace and Company

COPYRIGHT, 1953, BY
WILLIAM O. STEELE

*All rights reserved, including
the right to reproduce this book
or portions thereof in any form.*

first edition

LIBRARY OF CONGRESS CATALOG CARD NUMBER: 52-11964

PRINTED IN THE UNITED STATES OF AMERICA

J   70107

Fiction
S
Lib.
Sci.

FOR JOHN A. CHAMBLISS
Jurist, Legislator, Arborist, Agriculturist,
Historian, Promoter, Equestrian, Inventor,
and friend.

Wilderness Journey

Chapter One

"THAT'LL BE HIM a-coming yonder, Flan," said Uncle Henry.

Flan peered through the mist. The fog rose over the Holston River like a white wall. He couldn't see a thing but the dripping bushes growing on the river bank on one side of him and the lank figure of Uncle Henry standing a little way in front of him.

But there was the sound of splashing across the river. Someone was crossing the ford. And presently a dim shape loomed up through the fog near the bank.

"Howdy!" called out a man's voice.

"Howdy!" answered Uncle Henry. "Be that Chapman Green?"

"It be," the voice replied. "Leastways it was Chapman Green when I started. In this here fog, a body's liable to get turned around and be somebody else afore he knows what he's about."

The man chuckled and slapped his horse. "Git on there, Meg." He was leading another horse.

"This here's my brother's boy, Flanders Taylor," said Uncle Henry. "He's a-going with you over the trail. When you get to the French Salt Lick, his pappy'll pay you for your trouble."

"Aye," said the stranger and he squinted down at Flan. "Will he give me a heap of trouble?"

Flan stared back. He was a little disappointed in Chapman Green. "Maybe he's a Long Hunter like Uncle Henry said," he told himself, "but

4

he don't look like much. He's as dried up looking as a last year's persimmon."

"Well, he ain't too handy," said Uncle
Henry. "He don't own no rifle and I reckon
he don't know how to use one. He ain't much
hand with a ax or a knife. But he's good at his
letters. He can read like a preacher. He's been
sick a right smart, and I reckon that's how come
he's so backward."

Flan gazed miserably at his moccasins. He
reckoned Uncle Henry had to tell Chapman
Green about his shortcomings, so that too much
wouldn't be expected of him on the long journey over the Wilderness Trail. But how Flan
wished he wouldn't.

He sighed deeply. It was all true, though. He
wasn't much count. He couldn't shoot a rifle.
He couldn't chop down a tree and rive it neatly
into shingles. He didn't know how to skin a
deer or a bear, nor how to hang the meat to dry
or tan the hide so it was soft to the touch. He
wasn't much use for anything but chopping the

weeds out of corn. Even his mam said he was unhandy as all git.

Chapman Green laughed as he swung down off his horse. "Me and the lad'll make out," he said. "I'll take care of him. He can read to the painters at night, so they'll leave the horses be."

The cold mist from the river swirled up around Flan. He shivered. He wished they'd get started. Uncle Henry might change his mind and not let him go with Chapman Green. Flan didn't want to stay here on the Holston with his kin. Aunt Sara worried over him all the time, poking him with her long fingers and looking at his tongue. She fed him bowls of bitter herb tea and rubbed smelly salves on him every night.

He wanted to get away over the mountains by the Wilderness Trail to the French Lick where his own folks were. He wanted to be with his mam and pap and see his brothers and sister once more.

Uncle Henry laid his hand on Flan's shoulder. Flan shivered again with cold and excitement.

"What ails you, Flan?" Uncle Henry asked

6

sternly. He bent over and looked at the boy. "Have you got the shakes? Be you coming down with a fever?"

"I'm just cold, Uncle Henry," answered Flan quickly. Oh, he couldn't stay here now.

Chapman Green squatted in front of Flan and gave him a searching look. "Ain't nothing ails the lad," he told Uncle Henry briskly. He pushed Flan gently toward the horse in the rear. "Flan, you hop on this horse. Me and you are going to ride as far as the Blockhouse. Then we'll ride shanks' mare. The best horse in the world, don't need feeding or stabling." He winked at Uncle Henry.

Flan sat stiffly on the horse. He wasn't much used to horses. His mam thought walking was healthier for a sickly boy. The few times he'd ridden a horse had been behind his pap or one of his big brothers.

Green climbed easily onto his horse's back and moved off. Flan was worrying about how to make his mount start, but his horse followed the other off through the fog.

8

"Fare ye well, lad," called Uncle Henry after him.

"Good-bye, Uncle Henry," Flan answered weakly.

"If'n you git the shakes afore you git to the Blockhouse, stay there. I'll come fetch you," yelled Uncle Henry.

"I will," Flan promised. But in his heart he vowed he wouldn't stay at the Blockhouse, if he shook plumb off the horse. He had set out on this journey now and nothing would make him turn back. Aunt Sara would never get another tonic down him.

Ahead of him he could hear the dull thud of Chapman Green's horse's feet. He wanted to get his horse up a little bit so he could ride beside Mr. Green, but he was a little afraid of trying. He might give this old fellow a kick and he'd go scooting over hill and dale and end way up in the Virginny Valley.

It was mighty lonesome riding along in the wispy fog with only the sound of the river shoals beside them and the thudding of the hoofs breaking the silence of the early September morning. When they turned away from the river, Mr. Green began to sing in a loud mournful voice. He sang *The Twa Sisters*. Flan thought it was a very sad song.

The Long Hunter stopped singing and reined his horse in to drop back beside Flan. "How come you didn't go to the Lick with your folks?"

"I was all set to go, but I took down with the quinsy and Mam was a-feared to have me traveling," Flan answered, remembering how sore his throat had been. "I stayed on with my uncle and aunt. They aimed to have me go with the Johnsons last week, but Aunt Sara said the weather wasn't fit for travel."

Mr. Green nodded and scanned the trail ahead. The trees rose up tall around them. The thinning fog floated among the tree trunks.

Flan studied Chapman Green as they rode along. The Long Hunter was dressed in buckskins, with his hunting shirt belted in the middle and a knife and a tomahawk thrust into the belt. A worn and dirty-looking coonskin covered his head, a powder horn hung over one shoulder and a shot bag over the other. He rode his horse with one leg drawn up across the animal's back and his rifle resting on this leg.

"How old be you?" asked Chapman Green abruptly.

"Ten," answered Flan. He was small for his years, he knew. He could feel his thin shoulder blades sticking out through his linsey-woolsey shirt as he spoke. He wished he'd worn his buckskin shirt that he carried bundled in his blanket. It made him look bigger.

The trees thinned and fell away from the trail. The sun burned down and the last of the fog vanished. Now they rode through meadows and fields. The grasses along the trail were golden brown and the pinkish-purple heads of joepye-weed stood up tall and bright in the creek bottoms. On the hillsides the oaks and hickories were still a dull green, but sourwoods and black gums flamed among them. A killing frost was due any night.

Flan felt better now that the sun had warmed

him good. He was getting used to the rhythm of the horse under him, and he no longer clutched its neck when the beast stumbled or swayed off the trail.

"That's Matthews' place," he told Mr. Green, pointing. "They got ten slaves. They been here a good spell, since 1773, the year after I was born."

"Looks like they aim to stay on a while longer. They been clearing new ground." Mr. Green nodded toward a field covered with stumps and a burning pile of recently felled trees.

"Their oldest boy's gone to Virginny to get his schooling. He aims to be a lawyer. My mam thinks I ought to be a lawyer," Flan said shyly.

Chapman Green looked thoughtful. "There's a heap of money to be had in the law," he said at last. "But then there's a heap of places a man can be where money ain't much use to him. Take the country I just come from. Nothing but bears and painters there, and I never seen one of them varmints that put much store in silver and gold."

Flan was startled. "You mean over at the French Salt Lick?"

Mr. Green laughed. "Naw, I mean way over to the west, in Chickasaw Injun country. Ain't no settlers over there. The country's all as wild as rattlesnakes."

Flan rode along in silence. Money might not be much use out in that country, but he figured he wouldn't be much use either. He shook his head. Things would probably be as bad at the French Salt Lick as they had been here at home on the Holston River.

He hated to think all his life he was going to be so all-fired awkward and thick-headed. It seemed like he just never could do the right thing. His brothers all laughed at him and his mam babied him for it. She said the Lord would look after him and that was why He made Flan so quick at his books. But it wasn't his books Flan wanted to be quick at.

He wanted to be good at all the things his brothers were good at. He wanted to shoot a rifle and throw a tomahawk so that it turned over in the air and hit the mark with its blade up. He wanted to be able to go out in the woods and not be afraid, to know that he could take care of himself no matter what dangers might be waiting for him.

Mr. Green began to tell Flan how he happened to be going to the Lick. "I come back from Chickasaw country by the French Lick. Some folks over there calls it Nashborough now," he added. "James Robertson, he was there, and he asked me was I going home. I got a sister living in Carter's Valley, and I reckon that's the nearest thing to home I've got."

They stopped to let the horses drink at a little spring.

"I told Jim Robertson I was headed that way, and he asked me would I fetch some horses and a load of powder back to the Lick. And I allowed as I would. So here I be with the horses, and yonder's the Blockhouse. I git the powder there."

Flan looked ahead. He'd been to the Blockhouse a few times before. It was a two-story log cabin with the second story sticking out over the first. He reckoned it would make a pretty good fort.

Flan could see the loopholes, through which the men inside could fire their rifles at attacking Indians. The loopholes were chinked up now, but it gave Flan the shivers just to look at them. He'd been in a couple of Indian raids a few years back, and they were scarifying sure enough.

They rode into the yard and Flan slid to the ground. For a minute he was a little dizzy without the jolting movement of the horse, but he was glad to have solid earth under his feet again.

"Tie the horses over there where they can feed a bit," Chapman Green told the boy. "I got some business to tend to here."

Gingerly Flan took the horses by the bridle and led them to the spring at one side. While he was tying them to some bushes, one of the horses lifted its lip and showed its great yellow teeth. Hastily Flan backed away from the animal. He glanced over his shoulder to see if Chapman

Green had noticed, but the Long Hunter was not in sight.

Flan turned back to the horses. "I dast you to bite me," he muttered.

He moved over into the shade of a sugar tree and sat facing the house. In a few minutes Chapman Green appeared at the door of the tavern. "Come on in, if you're a mind to, Flan. I'll be here a little spell."

Flan shook his head. He didn't want to be in there under the curious stare of folks. From where he sat he could see a piece into the dim interior and hear the sounds of laughter and talk.

He sat under the maple tree for quite a while. He was beginning to get stiff from the unaccustomed riding and hungry enough to eat jaybird stew. He got out the hunting knife his father had given him when the family left to go to the French Lick, and inspected the blade. It was a mighty fine blade. At least he reckoned it was, it was all bright and shiny looking.

So far Flan hadn't used it for a danged thing

except to cut a willow twig and make himself a whistle two days ago. He took the whistle out of his shirt and blew on it. It didn't make much noise. Maybe fall wasn't the right time of year to make a whistle. Or maybe he hadn't made it right. He slipped the bark off the whistle. The notch ought to be deeper. He gouged at the twig and the knife slipped and gashed his finger.

He cried out and stuck his bleeding finger in his mouth. It wasn't a deep cut, but it made him mad that he was so clumsy with the knife and couldn't make such a simple thing as a whistle. In disgust he threw the pieces of willow into the bushes and sheathed his knife.

Just then Chapman Green came out of the tavern door with two bowls in his hands. A girl followed him with a pitcher and pewter mugs.

"I reckon we'd best have a meal afore we go," he told Flan. He grinned and sat down cross-legged on the ground. "I like to eat my vittles out in the open air, same as you do."

He handed Flan a trencher of greens and venison and the girl poured him a mug of buttermilk and broke off a big piece of ash cake. Flan mumbled his thanks.

He watched as Mr. Green brought out his knife and ate with it. Flan got out his knife, too, and stabbed at the deer meat. At home he'd always eaten with a horn spoon, though his brothers all sat around the table popping their skillfully laden knives into their mouths.

When they had finished their meal, the girl came out again to take the bowls and mugs. Mr. Green cut himself a sliver of maple and went into the tavern picking at his teeth.

In a moment he and another man brought out on their shoulders two kegs made of sections of hollow log with a deerskin tied tightly over each end. The man helped the Long Hunter adjust the quilts under the wooden pack saddle and then hoist the casks up onto the horses' backs.

The newcomer stepped back as Mr. Green began to test the straps and tighten the thongs around the horses' bellies. "You mean you're a-going on?" he asked. "You'll not be waiting

18

for the party Jeff Haines is a-getting up to leave in the next ten days? It'll be big enough to scare the war paint off any Injun between here and Jim Harrod's Station."

Chapman Green shook his head. "James Robertson'll be needing this powder. I'll have to travel slow with the boy there. I won't wait."

The other man looked at Flan a moment. "Well," he said with a shrug, "I'm glad it ain't me a-setting out over the trail with a half-dram lad and Injuns everywhere looking for scalps."

Chapman Green laughed. "My scalp's so old and flea-bitten no Injun would want it. Anyway I'd as lief lose my hair to Injuns as singe it off sitting in front of a tavern fire," he answered good-naturedly. "Giddup, Meg."

He moved off leading the pack train. Flan followed. He glanced back over his shoulder to see the man still staring after them.

"Well, one thing sure," Flan told himself. "James Robertson won't wait for his powder on account of me. I'll walk my legs off up to my knees to get there. Maybe I ain't so handy

19

with a rifle, but Mr. Green won't have to slow down for me!"

He took a deep breath and hurried after the horses.

Chapter Two

AFTER THE TWO LEFT the Blockhouse, the trail was wide and well-worn for a piece, but as the day went on, it got rougher and rougher. Flan was happier walking, for the ride had made him sore. But as they were crossing the ford at the North Holston River, he slipped and scraped his knee. The sun was hot and the way was uneven and he began to wonder if he would be able to keep his promise to himself after all.

He got a catch in his side and sat down on a log to rest for a moment, and when he looked up the pack train was gone. Desperately he sprang up and ran around the bend in the trail and caught up. After that he didn't pause again, but kept on doggedly. Chapman Green walked ahead, leading the horses and singing one sad song after another.

Once the Long Hunter stopped and peered at something in the soft earth beside the trail.

"Been a bear by here not too long ago," he told Flan. "A mighty fat one too."

Flan had sat down in the path as soon as Mr. Green had halted. He looked curiously at the tracks which were shaped almost like the track of a man's bare foot. He knew a bear's tracks when he saw them, but how did Mr. Green know this was such a fat bear?

"How can you tell if a bear's fat by its tracks?" he asked with interest.

"On account of all four tracks is showing," answered Mr. Green, straightening up. "A lean bear puts his hind feet in the tracks his front paws make. A bear that's been eating nuts all fall and got good and fat can't do that."

He jerked at the line. "Hey, Meg. Roddy, roddy doo," hummed Mr. Green.

They set off again. Flan walked beside Mr. Green and tried to take the same kind of springy steps. The Long Hunter moved down the trail as if his legs weren't part of him, but some kind of animal he was riding.

Mr. Green bawled out another ballad, which ended:

"He put the point towards his breast,
  The butt against the wall
Says, 'Here goes the life of three long lovers.
  God send their souls to rest.'

" 'Go dig my grave,' Lord Thomas he says,
  'Go dig it both wide and deep
And bury fair Ellen at my side,
  The brown girl at my feet.' "

He turned and winked at Flan. "Shucks, I been in Injun battles and ain't seen that many

killed. Yonder's Moccasin Gap, or my name ain't Chap Green."

He began to sing again. Flan wondered if he was going to sing the whole way to the French Lick. His brothers had always told him a man

had to be quiet out in the woods if he wanted
to stay alive. But here this Long Hunter bellowed like a freezing buffalo at every step.

Just ahead the mountains rose steeply on
each side of Big Moccasin Creek. Flan let his

eyes wander from the goldenrod and white snakeroot growing along the trail, up the hillside where scarlet sumac straggled among the rocks, to the top where tall pines leaned. It was a fine sight and he wondered if his older sister, Rosedel, had seen it when she went through here. She was a body who did love bright colors.

"We'll rest a bit here and get a drink," said Mr. Green "Ain't no need to bust ourselves wide open."

Flan flung himself down on the ground while the Long Hunter led the horses over the rocks to the stream to drink. When he came back, he sat down beside the boy.

"I mind the first time ever I come through Moccasin Gap," he said reminiscently. "Me and Slow Perkins come through here along 'bout this time of the year. We set down just like we're a-setting now. By and by a bear come sashaying by like he owned all this country round here. Slow said it wasn't right not to say hello to the bear, so he took up his rifle and fired. The ball took that old bear right across the shoulders and scared him most nigh to death, I reckon. He skedaddled through this Gap like greased lightning."

Mr. Green laughed and shook his head. "We was short of meat, so Slow and me took after him. But we hadn't gone far afore we seen we couldn't never catch that bear. He was making too good time for us, and we turned back. And right there on our heels was a whole fistful of the meanest looking Injuns I ever hope to see."

Mr. Green slapped his leg and rocked with laughter. Flan didn't laugh. He didn't see anything funny about Injuns.

The Long Hunter went on. "Me and Slow took off again. We passed that bear just about the time we come to the other end of the Gap. He was running right in front of Slow and I thought them Injuns would get Perkins sure, for he had to poke along behind that bear. But Slow just jumped plumb over him, like he was a huckleberry bush, without never missing his stride."

Flan grinned weakly. "What happened to them Injuns?"

"Why, they stopped to kill that bear. We left 'em so far behind they'd never caught up with us riding a thunderbolt." He chuckled and stood up. "Well, we best be getting on. We'd ought to get a good ways past Moccasin Gap afore night."

He tugged at the leather thong and the horses clopped along behind him. Flan groaned to himself, but he got wearily up and set out.

"What would you do if you met some Injuns in the Gap today?" he asked.

Mr. Green pondered a little. "I don't rightly know. Things are a little different. I got this powder for Jim Robertson and he needs it bad. I wouldn't want to just hand it over to the redskins." He grinned at Flan. "I'd have to think up something pretty desperate, I reckon. I don't figure on meeting any Injuns howsoever."

Flan hoped he figured right.

They crossed that creek and crossed it and crossed it. They went a little way along one bank, and the rocks got so thick they had to splash over to the other side. Then the hillside sloped down too steeply, and back they came. But in a little bit the cane grew so thick the trail crossed over again.

Flan struggled over the stones and through the muddy water.

He took off his moccasins and walked bare-footed, though the rocks hurt his feet and he slid a good bit where moss made the creek bottom slimy. Then a big snake went wriggling away right under his feet and he quickly put his soggy moccasins back on. Better to slosh along in wet shoes than have some varmint go off with his toes.

They passed a stand of tulip poplars where the Gap widened. Flan looked up and up to see the top of the tree where the odd-shaped leaves turned and rustled in the breeze. It would be fine to be a bird, he thought. Way up yonder there'd be no snakes or Injuns to bother a body.

"A woods of tulip trees pleasures me a heap," remarked Chapman Green. "Looky yonder at that one. It's nine foot through the trunk if it's an inch."

The tree was the biggest Flan had ever seen. The trunk rose straight up into the sky and not a knot in sight. What a dugout his brothers could make out of that tree! It'd be big enough to hold the whole Holston River settlement.

"Climate around here must be good for growing things, Flan," grinned the Long Hunter. "You and me ought to stick around for a while, sure enough."

Flan looked up and gazed at the man for a few minutes. It was true. Chapman Green was far from a big man. His arms were lean and muscular, but he was not tall. His frame was small compared to Flan's big black-haired brothers.

"I . . . I don't know how come me to be so puny," Flan stammered as they splashed through the creek. "I got three brothers and they're big and strong. Ain't a one of 'em under six feet, and the youngest just fifteen. Mam says I take after her family."

"Well, you ain't so all-fired puny," Chapman Green said kindly, his gray eyes twinkling in his wrinkled brown face. "Put a little meat on your bones and you'd be a likely sized boy, I reckon."

"I'm a heap littler than them," Flan insisted. "And they can do anything, shoot a rifle and throw a knife or tomahawk, and hunt, and skin deer, and do most everything you can think of." He sighed. "I'm so weakly I reckon I won't never be able to take care of myself in the woods or be good at hunting and things."

"Size don't count for much, Flan." Mr. Green spoke gently. "I'm a mite on the small side myself, and I've got along in the woods for nearly thirty year now. Since I was a tad, and my mammy and pappy died of the lung sickness up in Pennsylvania."

They came to a thick wall of cane, and the trail crossed the creek once more. "Why, Flan, you'll never make a lawyer. You've let them brothers argue you into believing a big man can do anything."

Flan pondered. Was it true? Did he always think of himself as too little to do anything? No, it wasn't only size. He just didn't seem able to pick up an ax and make it hit where he wanted it to, as his brothers did. He couldn't run as fast nor walk as far as they did. He was just all-fired awkward and that was that, he decided.

"If'n a fellow had to drop on a bear and mash him flat to kill him, why, size might count some then," laughed Mr. Green. "But it ain't so. A little man can get along in the woods fine. All he needs is a little sense. And if'n Injuns get after a big man, trees are going to look like mighty small covering. Many's the time I've been glad I could lie low behind a little smidgin of a tree and not give them redskins anything to shoot at. Just let the Injuns start a-shooting and the skinny trees that turn up!"

The trail led them beside the creek over damp, spongy ground, but it was wide enough for Flan to walk beside the Long Hunter. Mr. Green turned and grinned at Flan. "Now I mind once when being little saved me a heap of pain."

"I was a-walking along a trail and I kept a-hearing noises behind me—a rustling in the bushes and a sound mighty like footsteps. I looked around for an Injun, or maybe a wolf waiting for me to lie down and go to sleep, so as he could eat me.

"But I didn't see nothing. I kept on going, and in a spell I heard the noise right close up behind me. I jerked around, quick as a wink. My rifle hit against a big rock and went off. And there right behind me was the biggest, most monstrous bear in all creation, coming at me with his teeth all showing."

"A big 'un, huh?" asked Flan, hurrying a little so he could keep up and hear all of the story.

"Big as all outdoors," replied Mr. Green. "Well, there I stood with an empty gun and this old bear closing in on me. I didn't stop to pass the time of day, I can tell you. I turned round and run for my life. That bear took out after me a-breathing hot and fierce down my neck. And just as the two of us rounded a bend in the trail, another bear stepped out of the bushes. He was even bigger than the first one. I mistook him for a mountain, he was so big, but he growled at me and reached out his big old claws, and I seen my mistake. Well, there I stood between 'em. No way out, just right dab in the middle of the two biggest bears in Kentuck."

He paused. Flan waited for him to go on. "We'll mosey on up Little Moccasin Creek for a spell."

Flan noticed with surprise that they had left the gorge behind and were crossing a meadow which ran along the creek bank. A flock of blackbirds flew up at their approach.

"But what happened then?" Flan asked anxiously. "Did you kill both them bears? What *did* happen, Mr. Green?"

The Long Hunter glanced at the boy with a solemn look. "Flan, one of them bears ate me. I never did know which one it was, though."

For a moment Flan's mouth hung open in surprise, and then he began to laugh.

34

" 'Tain't a laughing matter, Flan," said Mr. Green seriously, shaking his head. "It ain't fitten for a boy your age to laugh at a man dying so painful. But see, lad, if I'd been a big man it would of been even more painful."

Flan giggled again. He wasn't so tired now, or at least he wasn't as long as Mr. Green talked to him and kept his mind off his legs.

He was keeping up pretty well. But now the hunter began to sing another ballad, the saddest yet. It made Flan's feet feel heavy as lead.

They were going between two mountains again and the trail was as rocky as ever. Flan gritted his teeth, glancing up at the sun now and then.

They couldn't in reason walk much further. Sundown and they'd camp. He'd have to keep his legs a-going till then. But he made sure the sun had stopped in the sky. It didn't seem like it would ever sink, but just hang there on the edge of the sky for the rest of creation.

"Cold supper for us," Mr. Green told Flan cheerfully. "We'll have game tomorrow night, but jerky's good enough for them that ate hearty at noon."

Flan didn't care whether they ate or not, he was so tired. And just as he thought he was going to drop from exhaustion, it was twilight. Way up on the top of the mountain overhead the pines were dark and fierce against a red sky.

"Yonder's where we're stopping," Chapman Green pointed. "It's just a little rise, not much bigger than a skeeter bite. But it's a divide, for a fact. Everything on this side runs into the North Holston River, and all the water on t'other side goes into the Clinch River." He added, "And tomorrow we'll be going into the Clinch River ourselves."

He pulled off to the side of the trail, unloaded the powder and hid it. Then he hobbled the horses and let them go near a cane patch, while Flan watched. He took his steel and flint and made a fire.

When the fire blazed up, he stuck four sticks in the ground near it. "Now take some of them dry leaves and stuff 'em in your moccasins and we'll hang 'em on the sticks to dry."

Flan did as he was told. His legs trembled with weariness, but the fire felt good and cheered him some.

"You get scald feet for sure wearing wet moccasins," Mr. Green explained. "You have to dry your moccasins out at night or they'll burn your feet like fire."

Flan took his dried meat and began to eat it, watching the fire. The jerk and ash cake which they had brought from the Blockhouse tasted pretty good, he decided, when he had finished and had a drink of water.

Mr. Green felt the moccasins. "I wish I had some bear grease. Next time I see a bear or a polecat, I'll kill it and grease these things good. Turkey fat will do pretty good."

Flan wrapped his blanket around him and lay down. He could hear the horses cropping the cane a little to one side. A night bird called way off down the hollow and another answered right above them. He thought about the water

37

flowing down this little hill, from one side into one river, from the other into another, and all of it going at last into the Tennessee. Suddenly he sat up.

"Mr. Green," he said hoarsely.

"Aye," answered the Long Hunter.

"Did you come as far today as you would have? Without me, I mean."

Mr. Green knelt by the fire putting the flames out with handfuls of earth. He stopped and rubbed his cheek. "Maybe so, maybe not," he answered finally. "I reckon we made pretty good time."

Flan lay back in his blanket again. The Long Hunter was lying. In spite of all his cheerful tales and talk of size not counting, he'd had to slow down for Flan. A ten-year-old boy and still he couldn't keep up. It was no use. He just wasn't good for anything.

He stared sadly up at the dark leaves above him, and fell asleep almost at once.

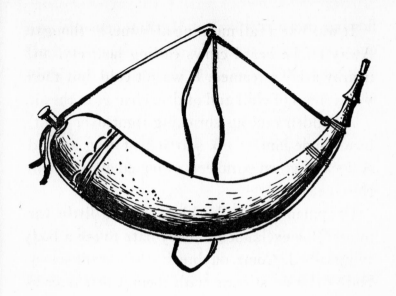

Chapter Three

FLAN AWOKE the next day and lay for a moment with his eyes closed. The ground made a hard bed in spite of the brush he had piled up to sleep on. When he moved his legs a little under the blanket, he could tell he was going to be stiff and sore. He could smell a fire and hear it crackling, and he could hear Chapman Green stirring around.

It was like a fall morning at home, he thought. Away off he heard crows calling hoarsely, and nearby a jay screamed. It wasn't cold, but there was a smell of chill and of dried leaves in the air.

A sudden raucous shrieking right over Flan's head made him sit up, startled, staring around. A flock of green parakeets swooped away among the tree trunks.

Chapman Green chuckled. "Them little varmints!" he exclaimed. "They hate to see a body lying a-bed. Come daybreak, they want everybody to be up stirring with them. Come over by the fire, Flan. I got something for you."

Flan struggled stiffly up out of his blanket and limped over to the fire. A skillet full of something bubbled on rocks over the flames.

"It's tea," explained the Long Hunter. "I made sure we'd need something to warm our innards this morning. We got to eat jerk again. I ain't got any sweetening for the tea, but it's got sassafras in it to flavor it up. And butternut bark for a tonic. And mullein leaf for croup and chest troubles." He frowned. "Seems like I meant to put in something else for chest sickness, but I can't recollect what it is."

"Sumac berries is good," said Flan, "and pine needles boiled with sugar. My Aunt Sara used lobelia and onions for the croup." He made a face.

Chapman Green stared at the boy. "You know a power of doctoring," he laughed. "But I reckon you don't know any remedies for snake bite or rifle balls, do ye?"

Flan was embarrassed. He reckoned he did sound like some old granny. He mumbled, "Snakeroot's good for snake bite, my mam always said."

"Best remedy for snake bite is to keep out of the snake's way," said the Long Hunter, stirring the tea with a stick. "I never knew a man yet to die of snake bite if he didn't get bit."

He held out a buffalo horn to Flan. "I aimed to make me another powder flask out of this. But I ain't had the time. It takes a heap of scraping, and I like my horns scraped thin inside and

41

out. Thin enough so the powder shows through it."

Flan took the horn. It had been scraped out some on the inside and it made a good cup. He held it up while Mr. Green poured tea into it. Oh, he'd be proud to keep this horn for his own. Maybe the hunter would show him how to scrape it and plug it up so he could make himself a powder horn. Then he could pretend he was a real hunter, who could shoot. He took a swallow of the brown steaming tea.

Mr. Green squatted down beside him. "Well, there's worse things than knowing a little doctoring," he said, blowing on his tea, which he drank straight from the skillet. "I reckon there's been many a hunter took sick out in the woods that wished he could remember what his mammy dosed him with. You've heard tell of Daniel Boone, him that widened this Wilderness Trail? Well, he's a good 'un in the woods. Knows a heap 'bout herbs and things and can cure most any ailment."

Flan chewed his meat and drank his tea. It

42

was better tea than Aunt Sara's. But breakfast back on the Holston River was better than this— eggs, and fried salt meat, and hot ash cake with butter and honey in a gourd, and a big bowlful of fresh milk. He swallowed down the rest of his jerk in a hurry, and tried to think of something beside food.

Mr. Green put out the fire carefully. Then he handed Flan his rifle. "A body can't be too careful. Keep this handy whilst I load up the horses."

Flan stared at the Long Hunter as he moved off toward the horses. Hadn't he heard what Uncle Henry said, about how Flan couldn't shoot? Mr. Green lead the horses to the place where he had hidden the powder and never looked back at the boy who crouched with the rifle across his lap and no idea what to do with it.

The long barrel gleamed dully in the red light of sunrise. Flan ran a cautious hand over the stock tracing with one finger the wavy lines of the wooden grain. He longed to curl his fingers around the trigger. Oh, how he wanted to shoot it!

His brothers all had their own rifles, and in the evenings they sat around the fire cleaning and polishing them and talking about what good shots they were. But they never let Flan touch the guns. On his tenth birthday his pap had let him shoot his rifle, and his brothers had shouted with laughter because he couldn't hold the heavy thing steady and had missed the cow shed.

He sighed. He'd never get to shoot another time, he reckoned. He doubted if he'd ever want to try, with them all standing around waiting to laugh at him. He'd like to ask Mr. Green to let him shoot, but maybe Mr. Green would laugh at him too.

When Mr. Green came back and took his rifle, Flan got up and they set off. At first he thought he wasn't going to be able to make it. His legs were all knotted up. But he limped on behind the horses, hurrying as best he could. As the day got warmer he felt better.

"This here's Troublesome Creek," Mr. Green said over his shoulder. "It's easy seen how it got its name." Flan, gazing up the winding trail in the rocky gorge ahead, could see.

They walked along a ledge above a deep clear pool. Long-legged bugs skated on the surface and deep in the still water Flan could see fish swimming.

When they came to the Clinch River, Flan thought they would have to swim, for it was a good-sized river and it looked deep. At the water's edge, Mr. Green showed him where a ledge of rock raised the bottom of the river, so they could wade across. The water only came to their knees, but Flan was afraid he would step off the ledge into the deep water. He walked close behind the horses and set his feet down carefully.

When they had crossed the river, they stopped to rest and pour the water out of their moccasins. A big persimmon tree grew near the trail and the orange fruits lay thick on the ground. Flan ate as many as he could reach, but one was not ripe and drew his mouth till he reckoned he'd never be able to talk again.

Mr. Green laughed at him. "Persimmons ain't safe till there's been a real heavy frost," he said.

In a minute he picked up his rifle. "See that blaze mark up yonder on that beech tree?" he asked. "Take this rifle and see can you hit it."

Flan's mouth dropped open in astonishment. As Mr. Green thrust the gun toward him, he put his hands behind his back. "I don't know how," he stammered. "I ain't never fired a rifle but once, and I didn't do no good then."

Chapman Green laughed. "I wouldn't give up on just one shot, was I you," he said. "A feller don't know what he can do till he tries a bit. Put the rifle barrel right up here in the crotch of this tree to steady it and see can you hit that blaze."

Flan took the rifle and did as he was told. His knees were shaking but he tried not to show how excited he was. He sighted down the barrel right at the middle of the white blaze. He took a deep breath and held himself as still as he could. Tensely he pulled at the trigger with two fingers.

There was an awful flash right close to his eyes and smoke rose up between him and the target. He jerked away, and then the gun roared. The bullet went humming off through the trees and the report echoed up and down the Clinch River gorge.

Flan pulled the gun out of the tree.

"Here," he muttered. "I can't do no good with it."

The Long Hunter took the gun. "You did all right. I should of warned you about the flash in the pan."

"I knew about it," said Flan wretchedly. "I just forgot. I ain't no good with a gun."

"Oh, I don't know," Chapman Green said absently. "It takes a spell to get used to a gun's ways. See here, Flan. When you pull the trigger, this here piece of flint hits that piece of metal there, with all them little grooves in it. That makes a spark, see, and the spark falls down in the powder in the pan, because the flint knocks the cover off the pan too, see?"

In spite of himself, Flan looked. A heap of things happened when you pulled the trigger.

He was astonished at all the mechanism in the rifle lock.

"The powder catches fire, and that's what makes that flash and smoke. It's apt to give a body a start till he's used to it. Next time you shoot, it won't bother you. But you got to be still when it happens, else you won't hit what you're shooting at. The fire in the pan goes through a hole into the barrel and fires the powder there, and that's the powder that sends your ball a-flying out. So don't wiggle an ear after you see the flash in the pan, and your ball will hit the mark every time."

The Long Hunter smiled at him. "How about trying again?"

Flan didn't want to. He hated making a fool of himself. Even resting the gun in a tree he couldn't hit the mark. But he wanted to do what Chapman Green wanted him to. Not many men would take the time to try to show a muddle-head like Flan how to shoot.

"All right," he said at last.

In a few swift movements, Chapman Green

48

had filled the pan with powder, poured more powder into the gun barrel, laid a lead ball on a cloth patch and rammed it home. Flan groaned to himself. Even if he ever learned to shoot, he'd never learn to load.

He took the rifle once more. He wasn't shaking now. He didn't have much hope of hitting the blaze, but he aimed as carefully as he could. Using his forefinger as Mr. Green had showed him, he pulled the trigger gently.

He squinted against the flash of the powder in the pan, but he didn't flinch. The roar of the gun was tremendous.

Mr. Green walked over to the mark and peered up at it a moment.

"Well, there ain't nothing wrong with your shooting eye," he called. "You hit it!"

Flan couldn't believe his ears. He ran through the bushes to stand by Mr. Green. Sure enough there was the bullet hole, a little to the right of the center of the blaze, but there it was. Flan felt like the top of his head would come off.

"I did it," he said wonderingly to the Long Hunter. "I hit it good, didn't I?"

"You sure did." Mr. Green grinned at him and began to dig the ball out of the wood. Lead was too precious to waste, and Mr. Green saved every bullet he could to melt down and use again.

"When we get to the Lick, will you tell my brothers how good I shot?" asked Flan.

"There's a heap of travel between here and the Lick," Mr. Green answered. "By the time we get there, I reckon you'll be a pretty fair shot. You can show them brothers of yours just what shooting is."

Flan didn't know just exactly whether he wanted to do any more shooting. He'd shot once and hit what he was aiming at. Next time he might not be so lucky. He'd hate to try again and make a fool of himself.

Still, he'd done it once. And Mr. Green had said he had a good shooting eye. Maybe he could do it again. Maybe sure enough by the time he got to Nashborough he'd be a fine shot. He pictured his brothers watching awe-struck while he stood up with a rifle and did a lot of fancy shooting.

The picture was almost too much for him and he jumped over three calico bushes on his way back to the horses. His legs weren't sore at all. He hardly noticed how steep and rocky the trail was when they started up Stock Creek.

"Is it all right to rest your rifle in a tree when you shoot, Mr. Green?" Flan inquired.

"Aye," answered the hunter. "Any time a tree's handy to steady your gun on, you'd best use it."

Flan nodded happily. He hoped there were lots of handy trees at the French Salt Lick.

The day wore on, getting hotter and hotter. Mr. Green sang and Flan toiled up the mountain path beside him, thinking about rifles and shooting. First he'd be proud of himself for hitting the mark this morning, and then he'd go cold all over thinking how next time he tried he might miss or do the wrong thing. Oh, he was always a-feared of doing the wrong thing.

Early in the afternoon Mr. Green handed Flan the thong with which he was leading the horses. "Here," he said. "Hold the horses a spell. We're a-coming to Little Flat Lick. I'll go ahead and see can I get us some meat for supper."

He went off quietly with his rifle, and Flan stood in the trail while the horses stamped and switched their tails. He was getting used to the horses. Now he put his hand on Meg and felt her hot soft hide. The mare turned her great head and looked at him thoughtfully.

It was hot. Flan could feel the sweat slide down his back and the rocks under his feet were warm right through his moccasins. He wished Mr. Green would come back. He listened for the sound of a gun, but none came.

Suddenly the Long Hunter was coming back down the trail toward him.

"The deer heard about me coming and went and hid," he called to Flan with a grin.

Flan gave Meg's head a jerk and started to meet him. When they had walked on a little way further, the valley widened. In a flat spot right at the head of the valley, Mr. Green showed Flan the Little Flat Lick, where there was a big spring that made the ground marshy and damp.

Animals had dug out big troughs in the ground as they rooted for the salt they craved. "Buffalo made them real big holes," Mr. Green explained.

"I ain't never seen a buffalo," said Flan.

"I reckon not. They left out of your part of the country a good while ago, soon as the settlers started crowding in. Ain't many around here any more, though maybe now and then they still come here. But up in Kentuck and over at the

54

French Salt Lick, there's a heap of buffalo there. And deer and every kind of game."

"That's how come my brothers wanted to go," Flan said. "They heard about the game, and my pap figured the land was better than it was on the Holston."

"Oh, there's game a-plenty," Chapman Green answered. "And it's rich land all right. I've seen cane growing so thick in the bottom lands, the creek couldn't go through. Had to go around."

"Gosh," said Flan.

"And grass grows so big, two buffalo can graze all day off of one blade."

Flan stopped and Mr. Green turned around to look at him.

"Oh, well, now maybe it ain't quite that big, Flan," he laughed. "But that's mighty rich land and good for growing things." He glanced up at the sky. "We'll make it through the Powell Mountain Gap this afternoon, I reckon, and I'll get us some supper then."

The sun was low in the sky when they reached the Gap. Flan stood panting on the mountain top and gazed down the steep winding stony path they had come up and wondered how they had ever made it. He raised his eyes and looked east over the tree-covered hills between him and the Holston River country.

"I've come a long way," he told himself happily. "There's a heap of walking behind me I won't have to do again."

But at the other end of the Gap, his heart sank. There before him again stretched the blue mountains and shadowed valleys, going endlessly off into the distance. There was half the world still to cover between here and the French Salt Lick. And it was all wild country. Danger of every kind lurked among those great trees. Who knew what lay ahead?

They descended the other side of Powell Mountain and went a little piece along a creek. Mr. Green picked out a camping place and told Flan to tie the horses where they could feed.

"I heard a turkey off that way a-hollering. I aim to have him for supper, if'n I can," he told

Flan, and he set off through the trees with his rifle.

Flan tied the horses and sat down with his back against a big rock. He watched a bat loop overhead after insects. The light was going from the sky. He peered down the dim trail and wished Mr. Green would come back.

The horses crunched cane and the creek made a tiny murmuring noise. Way off a whippoorwill called. Flan strained his ears. An owl gave a little quavering laugh right behind him.

Flan shrank against the rock. All his life he'd heard how Indians signaled to each other with bird calls. Maybe that hadn't been a turkey Mr. Green had heard at all, but an Indian scout notifying the other braves that a lone white man and a boy who had no rifle and couldn't shoot if he had were coming into the valley.

It was dark!

He pressed against the rock listening hard for Chapman Green's footsteps on the trail. He couldn't hear any definite noise, but the forest seemed full of little vague sounds that might be

Indians creeping closer to scalp him. Surely the Indians had Chapman Green or he would be back by this time.

Finally he could stand it no longer. He got silently to his feet and stepped out into the trail. He didn't know just which way to go, or what to do.

He walked slowly down the trail in the direction the Long Hunter had taken. He kept in the shadow at the edge of the path and tried to move as swiftly and silently as he could.

Once he stopped, startled at something, he didn't know exactly what. He turned his head to look back the way he had come. Something grabbed him by the shoulder and a hard hand pressed firmly over his mouth!

Chapter Four

FLAN'S KNEES BUCKLED and he made no resistance as he was drawn silently down into the bushes. The Indians had him! He would never get to the French Salt Lick. He would never show his brothers how he could shoot. He would never see his mam and pap again.

But gradually he became aware that some one was whispering to him and the voice was a familiar one. It wasn't the Indians who had him.

"There's a fire up the trail a ways. You stay right here and don't make no noise, whilst I go see who it is."

Chapman Green took his hand from the boy's mouth. "Now stay put, Flan. Don't come after me no matter what you hear," Mr. Green whispered. "And if I ain't back by daylight, strike out for the Blockhouse."

Then the Long Hunter was gone without a sound, melting into the shadows. Flan didn't even get to ask him so much as one question. Here he was left helpless with nothing but a knife to protect himself. And Indians camped up the trail!

He couldn't move. The thought of the cruel savages creeping through the black woods was enough to paralyze him. Sweat rolled off him, but his hands and feet were icy. He sat motionless on the dry leaves with a twig tickling the back of his neck. Something skittered through the leaves right at his side and he jumped a foot and listened to it leaping off into the darkness.

It was no use telling himself it was a rabbit. Every leaf that moved was an Indian coming closer. A late firefly was firelight gleaming on an uplifted tomahawk. Suppose in a moment now he should hear the horrible war cry and Chapman Green's screams as he died at the hands of the redskins?

He reckoned he'd never be able to make it back to the Blockhouse alone, an unhandy boy like him with no rifle. He'd probably never get a chance to start. The Indians would find him easily and scalp him before he could get out of the bushes.

He put his hand up to his dark straight hair, seeing it dangling from some Indian brave's waist. His arm struck a branch and set the bushes rattling and his heart pounding. No, he wouldn't keep alive long in the woods, awkward and un-thinking as he was, always doing the wrong thing.

Suddenly there was a shout out of the night. Flan started and the sweat poured down his face. Was it a war whoop?

Now it sounded like men talking. He strained to hear. What was happening? He dug his nails into his palms to keep from groaning aloud. He couldn't breathe.

Why in the nation hadn't he gone with Chapman Green? It would have been better to die being scalped than to sit here and wait to die of goodness only knows what.

And then there were footsteps on the trail and a voice called, "Come on out, Flan. It's all right."

For a moment Flan was too weak with relief to move or answer.

"Flan!" Mr. Green's voice was worried. "Flan, where be you?"

"Here," Flan answered finally, standing up among the bushes.

"Come along lively. It ain't Injuns a-tall. It's a white man, a trader feller named Rhea. And he's shot that turkey I was after and got it all cooked for us!" He laughed.

Now that the danger was past, Flan was tremendously tired and sleepy all of a sudden. He stumbled into the circle of the trader's fire and drowsily nodded his thanks when Mr. Rhea handed him a big turkey leg. He ate it while Mr. Rhea and Mr. Green talked. The last thing he remembered seeing was Mr. Green rubbing turkey fat into their moccasins. Then he was asleep.

He woke early next morning. He'd sort of hoped he wouldn't be so stiff and sore this day, but as soon as he sat up in his blanket his muscles started aching.

The Long Hunter was already up and in a few moments the trader threw back his fur robe and sat up. He and Flan went down to the spring together to get a drink. They ate the remains of the turkey for breakfast.

"I got meal for ash cake," said Mr. Rhea. "But there's no use wasting it when we got turkey breast. We may need that meal afore long. Game's scarce." Chapman Green agreed and handed Flan a piece of the breast. The white meat was dry and fine-textured and it was almost as good and satisfying as bread. Mr. Rhea had gathered some beechnuts and he gave Flan a handful to eat as they walked.

While the trader was getting his truck together, Mr. Green handed Flan his rifle.

"Here. There's a big knot over on that hickory tree. See if you still got that shooting eye."

Flan took the rifle, but glanced uneasily at Mr. Rhea. The trader was busy getting his pack onto his horse, and seemed to be taking no notice. Flan picked out a handy tree to steady the rifle and aimed carefully.

He fired three times. The first time he hit the tree near the knot. The second time he missed completely. The third time he hit the black knot square in the center.

"Now ain't that fine shooting for a lad that never fired a rifle but once up till yesterday?" asked Mr. Green proudly.

Flan swelled up fit to burst.

Mr. Rhea came and examined the knot. "How come a boy like you ain't learned to shoot afore this?" he asked.

He looked at Flan accusingly, and Flan felt himself turning red.

"Well," Mr. Green answered for him. "He's got some big brothers that figured they could shoot so good he didn't have no call to learn how. When he tried, they like to bust theirselves open laughing at him, instead of helping him do better. But he's a natural-born shot."

Mr. Rhea shook his head. "Aye, when brothers laugh at brothers, they're bound to come to grief sooner or later. When I was a boy I laughed at my oldest brother for a story he told, till he up and left home. And now I know it was the truth he spoke and I ain't never laid eyes on him again to make amends."

He looked very doleful. Flan wondered if he was going to tell what the story was that the brother had told. The horses were ready now, so they set out down the trail.

"My oldest brother was a hand for traveling in strange parts," said Mr. Rhea slowly. "He come home with tales about this and that, and we always believed him. All except me, that is, and

I'd laugh at all his tales and say they were lies. It was because I was the same as he was, I reckon, and I was a-hankering to be off to new lands myself.

"It made me fiesty to hear him come back and tell of those places, and me not able to go and see 'em. So no matter what he told I'd laugh and hold my sides and say it was the tallest tale I'd ever heard."

He sighed and ate a beechnut. "So when he come home a-telling how he'd found bones as big as cabins, I 'lowed that was the best tale of all. I laughed till I cried. I told my other brothers and my relations and all the neighbors he was addled in the head, for he claimed he'd seen the bones of animals as tall as mountains.

"I laughed at him and guyed him till the others took it up, and every time we'd see him coming we'd yell, 'Oh, Jack'—for that was his name, Jack—'Oh, Jack, we just seen a 'possum twelve feet tall down at the spring!' Or some such thing. And after a spell he got so riled up, he left the cabin one day and vowed he'd never come back."

"Didn't you never see him again?" asked Flan.

"Never laid eyes on him till this day," answered Mr. Rhea. "But two, three years ago, when I was up in Kentuck country with another feller, we come on a marshy place there. And lying about on the earth was the biggest bare bones I ever hope to see. Rib bones so tall a man could stand inside 'em and stretch his rifle up as far as he could and still not touch the top. Leg bones taller than a horse. It fair give me a turn to stand in that quiet place with all them great white bones lying about. Me and my partner left out of there, but I stayed long enough to know my brother'd been telling the truth."

"You never seen any of them animals alive, did you?" asked Flan a little fearfully.

"No, and I hope I never do," answered Mr. Rhea fervently.

"What kind of critters do you reckon they was?" asked Flan.

67

"Oh, now, game grows to right good size in Kentuck," spoke up Mr. Green calmly. "I expect those was a couple of rabbits or squirrels some wildcat had for his supper and left the bones there in the swamp."

He grinned at Flan and Flan grinned back.

They made good time for the rest of that day and all the next. Flan was proud because he could keep up with the two men. They never had to slow down or wait for him at all. Or anyway he didn't think they did. And his muscles were toughening up. After a day's hard walking he would be plenty tired and his legs stiff, but they were never sore any more.

Mr. Green made Flan take a few shots with the rifle whenever they stopped to water the horses or for a meal. He hardly ever missed now. Mr. Green said it was time he learned to load.

"Put the powder in the pan first off. That way you ain't apt to forget it," the hunter explained. "Just a dab, then close the pan cover."

Flan could see that it wouldn't take much,

for the pan was shallow, but he was worried about how much to pour in the rifle barrel.

"Now there's some that measures the powder they put in the barrel," Mr. Green went on. "That's fine, if you got all the time in creation. But if Injuns is a-coming or a bear, you'd be better off pouring the powder straight from the horn. So you might as well learn that way right off."

Mr. Green placed the small end of his powder flask in the muzzle and shook powder down it once, twice. "A couple of quick shakes like that. It ain't hard once you get the hang of it."

He reached inside his shot pouch and took out a patch made of coarse tow cloth. "It's best to keep you a few patches already cut out, but they're no trouble to make. Put one on the muzzle and center the lead ball on it. Then you start it down the barrel with your thumb, like this. And push it on down with your ramrod. Not hard, mind you. Just send it down easy like till it'll just touch the powder. Now you try it."

Flan tried. He stuck his tongue out and

worked hard. The day was hot and water dripped from his forehead and chin till finally Mr. Green laughed.

"You can't fire a rifle with wet powder, Flan," he teased, and Flan grinned at him.

But he sweated on and loaded his gun. After that he loaded every time he shot. He made mistakes sometimes, but he didn't mind. Mr. Rhea said he'd never be a fine shot because his eyes were too close together. Flan knew he would in time. He was getting used to the rifle now, and the quick jolt of the recoil against his shoulder was a good feel. If he sometimes poured too much powder in the pan so that when the cover closed the extra powder was knocked to the ground and wasted, Mr. Green never said a word.

At first Mr. Rhea watched him shoot, shaking his head sadly at every mistake the boy made. Then as Flan improved, Mr. Rhea didn't pay any more attention to his practice.

Mr. Rhea was a strange-looking man with narrow green eyes, and he didn't miss a thing along the trail. He was always on the lookout for something a little different, a little odd. He showed Flan queer rock formations, double leaves, a tree strangled to death by a vine, a hollow sycamore where swallows nested by the thousands. In his shirt he carried a white squirrel fur, the dried wing of a bat, some big brown beans with a sweet smell.

Flan liked the things Mr. Rhea showed him, but he didn't like to listen to the trader's tales. They were always sad or scary, about people who got drowned or snake-bit or killed by Indians. Sometimes it seemed like Mr. Rhea was the gloomiest man in creation.

His pack horse's name was Stella. He had named her that because she had a star on her forehead and once a man had told him that Stella was Latin for Star. She was a tall bony horse, as odd-looking as her master, with a funny patchy coat, but Mr. Rhea said she was the smartest horse in the States.

The third day they traveled with Moses Rhea was as hot a day as Flan ever remembered.

He struggled along the trail up and down the rolling hills with his linsey shirt clinging to his back. He was grateful for every patch of shade and cool stream they came to. The horses too lingered at the springs, their hides dark with sweat.

Mr. Rhea tugged at Stella's lead thong. "She's skittish today," he explained. "She smells Injuns for sure."

"She smells a storm more likely," said Mr. Green, and Flan hoped he was right. The very thought of meeting a band of Indians turned him to stone. He'd never be able to run from the savages. He'd do the wrong thing and get them all killed.

Sure enough in the early afternoon dark clouds billowed up in the sky to the southwest. Lightning flashed in the black sky and distant thunder grumbled, but the day stayed as hot as ever.

"We'd ought to make it to Cumberland Gap by night," said Mr. Green. He scanned the sky. "We'll get wet afore we get there, I reckon, but I won't mind. I'm as dry as the old well right now."

They walked on steadily. Flan felt baked, he was so hot. He drank at every spring they came to, and still, ten paces along the trail, his mouth would be as parched as ever. To their right the long blue line of the Cumberland Mountains stayed in sight but came no closer. Mr. Green quickened his pace, and Flan set his teeth and forced his legs to move faster.

Then the wind came whistling over the hills and hit them sharply as they trudged along. Brown and yellow leaves flew through the air and the dust swirled about their legs.

As they came to the top of a hill, the wind roared through the valley below them, bending the yellowing tops of the trees and making a wild noise. A great limb broke from a hickory tree and fell to the ground just behind them. Flan jumped, thinking it might be Indians. He knew he was too tired to run.

He drew in great breaths of the cool air. It was sweet with the smell of coming rain and the forest was alive and excited. Every leaf and twig spun and fluttered in the wind. A flock of pigeons flew over, were caught and hurled through the sky by the great gusts of wind. A buck and two does splashed across a creek and into the shelter of a thicket.

The Cumberland Mountains loomed right overhead now, gaunt and dark, and the gloomy thunderheads piled up. A spattering of rain fell and a flash of lightning split the sky.

The thunder growled and rumbled constantly and the wind blew so Mr. Green had to shout to them, " 'Tain't much further to the Gap, now. There's a cave there I know of. We can sleep dry in there."

Flan hoped it wasn't far. It was so dark he could hardly see to walk and the wind was so strong that when it hit him he staggered. They were going uphill now. He pulled himself along by the bushes that grew close to the trace.

"Here it comes," shouted Mr. Rhea and began to run.

Flan heard the new noise, a deeper roar than

that of the wind and saw the white mist of rain come driving toward them through the twilight. Then it was on them, pounding against the side of the mountain like horses' hoofs. It fell on him in a drenching torrent, and in a minute he was wet to the skin. The rain stung his eyes and he stumbled forward, blinded, frightened, and half-drowned.

Chapman Green guided him by the shoulder. "Come on," he shouted.

They stumbled on. Flan could hear his sobbing breath and his chest felt like it was splitting for lack of air. In the next lightning flash he could see the mouth of a cave in front of them.

"Here," shouted the Long Hunter. "Hold these horses, Flan, whilst we get the powder in the cave."

Mr. Rhea had already tied Stella beyond the mouth of the cave. Now he came back and the two men quickly unloaded the powder and disappeared into the black hole in the rocks.

Lightning and thunder ripped through the

sky. The horses shuddered and tossed their heads nervously. It was all Flan could do to hold them. In the flashes of lightning he could see the foam on their great mouths. He had thought the horses were his friends, but now he scarcely recognized them in these huge wild beasts who reared and whinnied and jerked at the reins.

In a moment Mr. Green took the thongs from his hand. "I'll tie 'em over yonder," he shouted, nodding to a place below the cave. Flan didn't wait to watch but scooted into the entrance. It was so low he had to stoop to keep from bumping his head.

Mr. Rhea was squatting on the floor of the cave holding a blazing splinter in his hand for a torch. Chapman Green came lumbering in, all bent over.

"I tied them horses good," he announced. "I hope you tied Stella pretty stout, Rhea. All this thunder and lightning's liable to send all three of them nags straight over to Chickasaw country. We don't want to have to spend tomorrow looking for 'em. Not but what the critters wouldn't break a leg sure getting down this mountain in the rain."

Mr. Rhea held his splinter higher and looked around. "Some friends left us a fire in here," he said in a strange voice. "Still a-burning."

Mr. Green checked his rifle, putting fresh powder in the pan. Then Flan watched as the two men examined the floor of the cave, especially the sand over to one side where a little stream flowed from the back of the cave and then out the mouth.

Chapman Green straightened up. "I reckon I'll go outside and take a look around for them friends," he said at last. "It was neighborly of 'em to leave a fire, but they had no call to throw a broken arrowhead down for us to find."

Injuns! Flan began to shiver in earnest and crept closer to the fire.

"If they aim to come back and use this fire tonight, I aim to know about it before they get here," Mr. Green said as he went out.

Mr. Rhea began to walk around the cave

78

looking for dry sticks to use on the fire. He found a few and built up the fire a little.

"I'm a-going this way," he told Flan, indicating a passage with his torch. "I might find some more wood back there. You want to come?"

Flan shook his head miserably. But after the trader had disappeared, he wished he'd gone with him. The leaping flames made odd shadows on the walls of the cave, and the sounds of the storm came to him weirdly from outside. He hoped Mr. Green came back soon.

Finally he went to the front of the cave and crouched there, looking out into the night. The rain had slackened a good bit, but the lightning was dazzling bright and the thunder was deafening. He could see the dark shapes of the horses, Stella on one side, Mr. Green's horses on the other side, further away.

Suddenly there was a terrible blazing light all around him, a hissing, crackling sound and then such a roar of thunder that it seemed to fling him back into the cave. He pressed himself against the rocks and peered out. The light-

79

ning had struck a tree, a dead pine tree standing not twenty yards from the cave entrance. And in spite of the rain it was burning fiercely.

And then in the light from the burning tree, Flan saw Meg and Brownie. Terror-stricken the poor beasts reared and plunged, jerking at the halters that tethered them. Fiery splinters from the burning tree fell around them and on them. They shrieked and lashed out with their hoofs. Stella whinnied in alarm, but she was tied safely out of the way.

Flan knew in an instant that someone would have to loose the horses. If the lightning-fired tree didn't fall on them and burn them, they'd kill each other rearing and fighting that way.

"Mr. Green!" he bellowed. "Mr. Rhea!"

But he knew neither of the men could hear, nor get to the horses in time if they heard. The horses would be killed, and the powder they'd brought this long way would never get to James Robertson.

With a despairing cry, Flan ran toward the plunging, maddened horses.

Chapter Five

HE KEPT HIS EYES on Meg as he ran. She was the nearest, he would free her first. He circled wide to avoid the plunging hoofs, slipping and stumbling over the rocks. Once a branch, heavy with rain, slapped him across the face and sent him sprawling among the wet underbrush.

One of the horses screamed.

"I'm a-coming, Meg," he panted, struggling

on. His wet buckskins made him slow and awkward.

Finally he reached the spot where Meg was
tied. Just beyond, the fire roared and crackled.
He put up his arm to shield his face from the
heat. In the red glow of the burning tree the
horses looked as big as mountains. Their lips

were pulled back from the great yellow teeth
and their eyes rolled madly. Again and again
they reared before him and came plunging back
to earth. Those flashing hoofs could crush his
skull like a puffball.

Flan began to work at the knot, picking at
it with trembling fingers. He worked slowly for

he had to watch Meg, stopping often to duck away from the snorting, thrashing mare.

He couldn't seem to get hold of the wet leather and finally he began to claw desperately at the thong, wishing Mr. Green hadn't tied it so tight, or that Meg wouldn't pull it tighter every time he tried to loosen it.

He glanced up at the flaming tree, towering over him in the blackened sky. It couldn't burn much longer. The top at least was bound to fall in another moment, and they'd all be burned to death. He had to do something quick.

His knife! What a wooden-head he'd been! Frantically he snatched out his hunting knife and reached for the leather thong.

There was a sudden sharp crack that made him jump. A limb broke from the burning pine and hurtled to the ground. A big flake of blazing wood lit on his hand and he dropped the knife. Half-sobbing he crouched to pick it up, snatching among those wicked hoofs and at last seizing it.

He pulled himself up by holding on to Meg's

tree. He could feel it tremble as Meg jerked in panic. Her eyes were wild and staring, and foam fell from her lips.

He slashed again at the leather thong. A shower of sparks sent the horses shrieking and rearing worse than ever. He cowered back for a second, but then he was sawing away at the thong again, standing as far back from the horses as he could.

But the knife didn't cut. There was something wrong with the knife his pap had given him. It wouldn't cut the thong at all.

With a rush of relief he saw that he had got the knife blade turned around and was trying to cut with the dull thick backside. In an instant he turned the knife over and hacked at the leather.

Then Meg was free. He heard the hard sound of her hoofs on the rocks as she vanished. He turned to Brownie.

Brownie was wild with fear. There was an ugly red mark across his nostrils. In a frenzy he lashed out at Flan, his big hoofs grazing the tree to which he was tied. Sweating with fear, Flan thrust at the thong again and again, but he couldn't get close enough because Brownie bit at him.

Any moment that tree would fall. Desperately he lunged forward and slashed at the thong where it circled the tree. He cut it cleanly and jumped away. With a final terror-filled whinny Brownie sped away.

"Run, Flan! The tree! Run!" Chapman Green's voice from the trail was hoarse.

Panic-stricken Flan stood in the circle of glaring light. A moment before he had known the tree would fall on him. Now each way he turned, he was sure that was the way the tree would fall. He was trapped. He could not move.

Mr. Rhea called sharply from the cave entrance, "This way, Flan!"

His wet leather breeches were like iron clothes. His knees couldn't bend in them and they were heavy as bars of lead. He didn't know how he ever managed to make his way over the slippery stones to the mouth of the cave. It seemed like a year till Mr. Rhea grabbed his hand and pulled him inside.

There was a crash and a moment of wild flaming light and a million stars seemed to fly through the night. But he was safe. He lay on the floor of the cave panting and gasping until Chapman Green bent over him.

"Be you all right, lad?" he asked anxiously. "You ain't burnt?" He pulled the boy to his feet, asking again, "Be you all right?"

Flan shook his head. "I ain't hurt," he said finally, though there was a blister as big as a frog on the back of his hand.

They walked back into the room of the cave. Flan took off his wet clothes and sat wrapped in his blanket while Mr. Rhea brewed him a hot drink.

"Put some mud on that burn. It'll take the sting out. I ain't got anything for a burn but that," Mr. Green told him.

Mr. Rhea poured the tea into Flan's horn cup and explained, "I went off a-looking for dry wood and I come on a room just full of all

87

sorts of rock shapes. Curious looking as all git. I broke off an icicle for you, Flan." He handed over a small brown stalactite, sparkling in the firelight. "Time I got back here, I found Flan gone and heard them horses squealing and taking on. I never figured he'd get out of that alive."

"He's a brave lad," said Mr. Green. "I made sure the Injuns had you when I seen the fire and heard the horses taking on so."

He set a flat stone down in the edge of the ashes to brown the ash cake. "I come up the trail as quick and quiet as I could and there's the boy risking his neck to loose the horses. I said then he was as brave a lad as I ever seen. He's tough. A mite puny, but he's tough."

Flan listened sleepily, his heart pounding with pride. He'd done the right thing for once. He'd done a good thing, a brave thing. He'd risked his life and won out, and he was as tough as hickory. He reckoned he could do most anything out in the woods, shoot a rifle, rescue horses, anything.

"Well, I hope he's tough," said Mr. Rhea. "Out in this weather, all that rain, he's liable to take down sick in the morning. He'll have a fever sure." He fixed Flan with his eyes.

"The tea'll fix him up," Mr. Green answered.

"It'll be bad if'n he starts ailing," Mr. Rhea went on dismally. "We can't stay in this cave. Them Injuns is likely going to come back here any time now."

Flan suddenly didn't feel so tough. If the Indians came back tonight, there'd be a fight. Fighting Injuns was a heap harder than saving horses, he reckoned.

"Nay," answered the hunter. "They're long gone from here."

"And so are them fool horses, I reckon," said Mr. Rhea. "Most likely run plumb back to the Blockhouse. We'll be all day tomorrow finding 'em." He looked gloomily into the firelight.

Flan drank his potion. He wasn't such a woodsman after all. A Long Hunter like Mr. Green would have held those horses, quieted them, not lost them in the black wilderness. He reckoned he wasn't so tough after all. He couldn't even shoot a rifle real well, unless he steadied it in a tree fork.

He might as well be a lawyer like his mam wanted him to be, he decided, as he rolled over and went to sleep.

Chapter Six

THE NEXT MORNING Mr. Green went out hunting the horses. Flan stayed in the cave with Mr. Rhea. His head hurt, and he felt gloomy because he'd let the horses get away.

Mr. Rhea wanted to take him back in the cave and show him the rock formations he had found the day before, but Flan wouldn't go. He sat huddled by the fire and tried to keep the smoke out of his eyes while he ate his ash cake.

In a spell, a heap sooner than Flan had expected, there was the sound of hoofs outside and Mr. Green's voice urging Brownie and Meg along. He came in the cave in a few minutes, grinning and rubbing his hands.

"The rain brought a change in the weather, for fair," he exclaimed. "Inch of frost on the ground and gitting colder every minute. Most likely the Cumberland will freeze and we can walk over."

Flan put his linsey shirt on under his buckskins. He looked sober. He knew Mr. Green was teasing about the Cumberland River freezing. But they'd have to ford that river, and it would be almighty cold doing it.

They went outside. The sun shone brightly, though the wind was like a knife. Flan shivered, looking around at the hoar frost sparkling on the ground and the ice on the puddles in the rocks.

Brownie had a burn on his back. Mr. Rhea agreed to let Stella carry Brownie's load of powder and let Brownie carry the trader's pack till the burn was healed, since the pack was lighter.

As Mr. Green fastened the wanty around Stella, Flan came up close to him. "Mr. Green," he said softly. "I'm sorry I let the horses go. I never went to let 'em run off, but I just couldn't hold 'em."

Mr. Green stared around at him in amazement. "Well, I'll be danged!" he said at last. "Now who in the nation give you the notion you was supposed to hold on to them critters? I couldn't of held 'em myself. It was enough to save their fool necks. Besides," he turned back to the horse, "they ain't been on the trail long enough to know how to be really aggravating. They just run to the first cane brake and stopped. And that's where I found 'em."

He grinned. "A smart horse can slip off every night, even with a hobble, and keep you looking for him half the day. I been on the trail with horses that rode me twice as much as I rode them."

Flan felt a heap better right away. He stood there a few minutes, sort of hoping Mr. Green would tell him how smart he'd been and how brave, but the hunter didn't say anything else.

Yesterday's rain had washed big gullies in the trail and it was hard going. Rocks had slid down into the path, and mud spread a slippery coating over everything. The horses stumbled and slid and so did Flan. Even Mr. Rhea had trouble, but Mr. Green stepped on down the path humming about *Barbara Ellen*. Every now and then he would sing a verse and it was always the same one, about a pale corpse. Flan wished he'd sing something else.

Halfway down the mountainside a big oak lay across the trail. Mr. Rhea and Flan took the horses into the trees at one side and hid while Mr. Green scouted ahead.

"That's a fine place for an Injun ambush," the trader said to Flan.

But in a few moments Mr. Green hallooed for them to come on. Flan asked Mr. Rhea, "Be there Injuns about, do you reckon?"

94

"Well, now, you can't tell," Mr. Rhea answered. "This here is the Warrior's Trail and they don't hanker to have us use it. It's best to watch out for 'em. Them savages is always about."

"You mean this is an Injun trail?" Flan felt the hair rise on his head.

"Aye," Mr. Rhea nodded. "It was an Injun trail long before white men come here. The Creeks got to run up north and visit with the Shawnees, and the Shawnees got to come down and see is the Cherokees getting along all right. Injuns is great on visiting." He laughed.

"How come we use it if it's an Injun trail?" asked Flan, glancing over his shoulder.

"Ain't no other way to get into Kentuck walking that I know of," Mr. Rhea answered as they caught up with Mr. Green. "I wish there was. Couldn't be no worse than this 'un and it might be a heap safer for folks."

Flan walked on silently. His feet were wet and his toes ached with cold. Clouds came rolling up in the sky and shut out the sun, and the wind was sharper than ever. He noticed that many of the trees had turned yellow or brown overnight, and here and there a bush or vine was covered with blackened leaves.

"When all the leaves go, it'll be easy for the Injuns to see us coming a long way off," he told himself. He looked back over his shoulder once again. Trailing along at the end that way, he'd be the first one to get scalped when the Indians came creeping up behind them.

He hurried up to walk with Mr. Rhea. The trader had picked up a dead bird from beside the trail. It was a large bird with a yellow bill and odd white spots on its tail.

"Looky here, a rain crow. You hear him a-hollering when it's fixing to rain. I reckon he must of hollered hisself to death when he saw that storm coming yesterday." He threw the bird to one side.

They reached the foot of the mountain and began to follow the trail as it wound through a valley. The way was not so hard and the wind didn't blow so much. Presently they came to a creek. It was swollen almost out of its banks and Flan did not like the look of the roiling muddy water.

"I'll take the horses over the ford," Mr. Green said. "Rhea, you and the boy cross on that raccoon bridge. There ain't no need all of us taking a bath today, for we had a good one yesterday."

Flan looked where the Long Hunter pointed to a sycamore tree that had fallen across the creek. He'd never in this world get across it. He'd sooner wade the icy creek than try to foot across that slippery log with the water going in dizzying whirls below him. But he had no choice.

"You first, Flan," said the trader and gave Flan a little shove. "If'n you fall off, maybe I can fish you out."

Mr. Green frowned. "He ain't going to fall off. He's walked logs afore, ain't you, Flan?"

Flan nodded. It was true at home he walked log bridges sometimes, but folks at home had sense enough to put an oak tree over a creek, a good big one with bark rough enough for toes to get a hold on. And days when creeks were

97

swollen like this, Flan stayed home with his mam.

He fastened his eyes on the other end of the log and set his feet down on the smooth white trunk of the tree. He had to do it, he told himself fiercely, and do it he would.

Once he started he didn't dare stop.

"Yonder's a dead drowned coon," exclaimed Mr. Rhea, but Flan didn't turn his head. He just went steadily on and when he stepped off the log at last, he thought surely his legs would give way under him.

"I knew you was a fine log-walker," Mr. Green called from the middle of the creek, and Flan grinned at him.

The ground beyond the creek was low and marshy, and here and there the bottom land was flooded and turned into a shallow lake. They sloshed on through the icy mud and Flan began to think he'd lost his legs from the knees down. They had no feeling at all, and that was a help, considering the way they'd been hurting up to the time they got numb.

The wind began to blow like fury.

"It's fixing to snow, I reckon," said Mr. Rhea in his sad voice. "The lad'll get the chest sickness sure. I heard him coughing twice this morning."

Flan looked up fearfully. He hoped to goodness he didn't get sick. Mr. Green would take his powder on to the French Salt Lick and leave Flan with Mr. Rhea. Flan didn't think he could stand being all alone in the wilderness with Mr. Rhea and his dreary tales.

"It ain't going to snow," Mr. Green remarked as he glanced at the sky. "It'll warm some tomorrow." He turned to Flan. "You feel all right, Flan? You got the shakes?"

"No, sir," Flan answered, swallowing another cough.

"We'll be out of this lowland soon. You grease your chest good, when we stop to eat, and you'll be all right."

They left the flat bottom lands and began to climb through the mountains. When they stopped later to eat, Mr. Green got some bear's grease from the trader and made Flan rub it all over his chest and shoulders, as well as his legs and feet.

"Bear grease ain't much good," said Mr. Rhea. "Polecat grease is the only thing for a cough."

"Polecats are scarce—the four-legged kind anyway," replied Mr. Green shortly.

But Flan didn't cough any more.

By afternoon they reached the Cumberland River. The trail ran alongside the stream for a mile or so, and Flan had plenty of time to study the wide muddy river and wonder how in the nation they were ever going to cross it. Swollen as it was with the heavy rains, they'd never be able to ford it. And it was rising higher all the time.

Would they have to swim? Flan wasn't much better at swimming than he was at anything else. That racing water would send him swirling down to the Ohio River before he got his wits together.

But he'd do it. If Chapman Green said swim, he'd swim, though it meant drowning.

The river boiled and eddied in muddy swirls along the banks. Trees, branches, and all sorts of debris came whirling down the current. Once Flan saw a huge trunk shoot up out of the water like a monstrous fish after a fly.

Finally the trail dipped down to the river. Here they would cross.

"A trader and his horse drowned here at this ford last spring," remarked Mr. Rhea mournfully. "A river in flood is the meanest varmint there is."

Mr. Green studied the river in silence a few minutes. "Rhea," he said at last, "how about you swimming the horses over, while me and Flan raft the powder across?"

Mr. Rhea nodded. "We'll do well to hit the other bank a mile below here."

"Can't be helped," Mr. Green answered briefly. "But I never seen the like of them trees. I hope they don't give us too much trouble."

"Trouble!" exclaimed Mr. Rhea. "We ain't got anything but trouble. If'n we get across this river alive, the Injuns'll be waiting for us, I'll vow."

Mr. Green handed Flan the rifle and told him to go up the trail a piece and keep a watch for Indians.

"This here is the Injuns' crossing place too," Mr. Green told him. "I ain't aiming to raft any of 'em over with us, can I help it."

He took his ax and walked toward a group of small tulip trees. Mr. Rhea said he'd get some vines to use and Flan went back up the trail, swinging the rifle the way Mr. Green did. He found a rock and sat behind it, where he could see the trail leading down the river bank, but no one approaching could see him.

At first he felt very brave staring up the trail on the lookout for Indians. He liked to think he was helping as much as he could. Later he reckoned his fingers were so cold he couldn't pull the trigger if he did see a redskin.

Finally Mr. Green hailed him. When Flan

reached the water's edge, the raft lay in the water. Mr. Green was tying the powder casks to it.

"You ought to use another log," said Mr. Rhea. "Four ain't enough."

"Me and Flan ain't so over-sized," Mr. Green answered. "Four's plenty for us."

Mr. Rhea sighed. "Well, them vine lashings ain't much. I hope it holds together till you get over."

Flan looked at the raft. It was kind of small. And bark and vines weren't much to hold it together in all that rushing water. But Mr. Green just went on tying his rifle to the top of the pile of bundles.

Flan held the raft while the men drove the horses into the river. It took a lot of hard licks with a hickory to get them into the racing water, but once in, they swam quietly off downstream. Mr. Rhea held on to Stella's tail and in a moment they were around a bend out of sight.

Mr. Green gave Flan one of the two long poles he had cut.

"Here, Flan, it might take the two of us to get across." He paused and looked down at the thin-faced boy holding the raft. "Don't pay that crazy trader no mind. He just talks like that. This raft don't look like much, but it'll fetch us over. I don't figure we'll have any trouble."

Flan nodded and stepped aboard the raft. Mr. Green put a hand on his shoulder as he stood beside him.

"There's just this, Flan. If there's trouble, you'll have to look out for yourself. I got this powder, and I *got* to get it to James Robertson. Do you see, lad? I'll have to take care of the powder, and you'll have to take care of yourself." He pushed with his pole.

Flan heard the water gurgle under the logs, and then they were out in the churning river.

Chapter Seven

THE RIVER hit the raft so hard that it set the logs trembling from front to rear. Flan, standing at the front of the raft, was astonished to see how fast they flew along. He sat down suddenly, holding his pole. The logs strained at their vine and bark lashings and knocked against each other, sloshing water up over his feet. Flan was careful to keep his feet from between the logs.

The bank they had left behind moved swiftly further and further away. They were fair in the middle of the river now, and going faster every second. If the raft split open now, he'd never get back to shore.

He remembered how one spring when the Holston was flooded, a family of woodsies had drowned in the river trying to raft over. Mother and father and little children and all their truck disappeared under the muddy water and were never seen again. The logs creaked and bumped and Flan reached out a hand and grasped the casks of powder to steady himself.

This raft would never hold together. Mr. Rhea was right. Those vines would break and the logs would scatter and Flanders Taylor would drown and his brothers would never know he could load a rifle and fire it fair. The water gurgled and roared.

Up ahead the river was white and foamy. That meant hidden rocks or shoals. They were headed straight toward it. Chapman Green would never be able to get the raft through that rough stretch.

"Mind that log, Flan!" called the Long Hunter.

Flan jumped to his feet. A big log was floating beside them and with his pole he pushed it away as best he could. It was hard to stand on those wet shifting logs and push. It seemed like a long time before the log moved away.

He looked around for more logs. He was ashamed that he hadn't kept watch before, the way Mr. Green had told him to. He was ashamed of all the fearsome thoughts he'd had a few minutes ago. He was as bad as Mr. Rhea, always looking for the worst to happen. Chapman Green had said the raft would get them across all right and he reckoned Chapman Green knew more about it than the trader.

They were coming to the rough water. The river was choppy and dangerous looking, and a good many logs and stumps and other debris whirled and pitched in the boiling current. It was awful looking, but Flan raised his pole and steadied himself. If anything happened, he wasn't going to lie down in the water and drown without lifting a hand.

Chapman Green cried out a warning as they came into the rough water. The raft groaned and swung back and forth in the eddies. It bucked and wobbled like a wild thing, and suddenly swung around sideways in the stream.

The motion threw Flan back against the pile of baggage. The rifle barrel struck him a hard blow across his cheekbone and the pain filled his eyes with tears. When he could see again, he made out Mr. Green standing on the edge of the raft jabbing frantically with his pole at the logs. Two or three came crowding against them at once, knocking and bumping.

The raft rocked along swinging this way and that until Flan was as dizzy as a gadfly. He moved his eyes from the whirling water to keep himself from getting giddy, and he saw Mr. Green's rifle. When he had fallen against it, he must have knocked it loose someway. It lay teetering across the trader's pack. In another minute it would slide off the raft into the river and be lost.

Flan reached for it. He reckoned Mr. Green would rather lose his head in the river than his rifle.

Mr. Green yelled warningly again. Flan looked up. Dead ahead of them was a great log, half a huge tree. The raft hurtled broadside on to the log and reared up in the air. As Flan's fingers closed on the rifle barrel, the jolt sent him sprawling. A second later he slid into the water.

He was too surprised to do anything but hold tight to the rifle. He opened his mouth to yell but the muddy water filled his mouth and closed over his head. He still hadn't let go of the gun.

With a jerk he came to the surface, spluttering and gasping. It took him a minute to see what had happened, that the gun stock had somehow got wedged between the last two logs and saved him.

On the other side Chapman Green struggled to get the raft off the log. Flan let go the gun with one hand and clawed at the raft. The wet bark was slippery and he couldn't get a good hold with his cold fingers. The rough current dragged and tore at him, trying to pull him loose. If the rifle stock broke now, he was gone. He'd never be able to hold on to the raft.

He got a better grip on the wet log. He kicked out with his legs and tried to bring his knee up on the edge of the raft. But then his grip failed and his knee slid off. He grabbed wildly at the rifle. He hit the trigger and the gun went off, but he barely heard the report above the noise of the river.

He couldn't hold on here forever. The current was about to drag him off. His fingers were so numb he couldn't tell whether he was still holding on to the rifle or not. The water pressed in on him and it splashed in his face so that he couldn't get a good breath. It was either git up or give up. He just couldn't last much longer.

Again he reached out with his hand. He felt hurriedly along the log and found a rough place for a handhold. Straining he slowly lifted one knee over the end log and then his elbow and part of that side of his body.

He let go of the gun and clawed at the next log. Finding a hold he wriggled upward, pressing his knees in between the logs. He was out of the water now. He reached out and grasped the cask bindings. Trembling with weariness and gasping for breath, he huddled against the baggage and pulled the rifle toward him.

He was safe. He was full of muddy water and soaked to the skin on a day when the wind was sharp as a knife, but he was safe. He hadn't drowned. He was alive and breathing and as he lay on the rough logs, he reckoned he'd never be that scared again and live to tell the tale.

Suddenly the raft gave a lunge and plunged off the log. Flan raised his head and saw the Long Hunter lay down his pole and wipe his forehead on his sleeve.

"I made sure I'd left you behind in the river!" Mr. Green shouted.

Flan couldn't get enough breath to answer. Anyway Mr. Green turned back to his poling.

Flan was surprised to see they were getting near the opposite shore. The river made a slight bend here, so that the current swept them closer yet. Mr. Green began to pole furiously. Even in the chill wind, sweat poured off his face. Where his buckskin shirt clung to his back, Flan could see the muscles stand out as the Long Hunter strained and pushed.

A shout made him look up. Mr. Rhea was wading out to meet them and help bring the raft to shore. He looked gloomier than ever.

"It's the Lord's wonder them vines held," he said. "I seen the boy couldn't stay on the raft. How'd you get him back on?"

"He got hisself back," Mr. Green answered. "He saved my rifle, too. I seen it all, but I was fighting four or five trees, and I didn't have time to lend him a hand. One of them logs was a mind to get on board in spite of all I could do."

"That powder has likely got wet anyway," announced Mr. Rhea. "You'd of done better to carry it in deerhide wallets than them kegs."

Mr. Green shoved the raft a little further up the river bank.

"Flan, get after them horses. We don't want to go looking for 'em in this cane. There's two, three miles more of this brake. When you get back with 'em, you take your blanket to keep the wind off you. We'll build a good fire and dry out."

The horses weren't far off. They were eating cane and they didn't want to come back to the trail. Flan had to chase them. But he was shivering in his wet buckskins and he was glad to run a little and get warm.

He was glad to see the horses. He patted their rough sides and remembered how scared he'd been of them back at the Blockhouse. He wasn't scared now. He liked them. He'd risked his own life to save theirs. He'd saved the horses and Chapman Green's rifle. He'd looked after himself on the raft. He hadn't hollered for help. He could load a rifle and shoot it.

Maybe he wasn't so unhandy after all. He

wondered what Uncle Henry would think to see him now.

The next day was the seventh day since they had left the Holston River country. Flan lay in his blanket and shivered. The thought of getting up into that cold crisp air was more than he could stand. He could see the thick white frost lying on the fallen leaves.

Finally he got up and rolled up his blanket and tied it with a thong. Chapman Green called him. "Come along, Flan, there's a creek over here. We'll fetch water and have us some hot tea this morning."

Flan went with Mr. Green down to the creek. "Looky yonder," Mr. Green whispered, and nodded up the stream.

Flan looked. A big gray and black goose was swimming slowly down the creek, stopping to nibble the grasses that leaned out from the bank. Softly Mr. Green reached for his rifle and handed it to Flan.

"Wait till she gets even with that big sycamore, Flan, and then shoot her in the head," he whispered. "Careful, now, and don't fire too soon."

Flan was so excited he never noticed he didn't have a tree to steady the gun. Slowly and cautiously he raised the gun. Carefully he sighted along the barrel as the goose came swimming gently toward the sycamore tree. Now he could see the little beady eye as it turned its head.

He pulled the trigger. He heard the report and saw the flash and smoke, but he didn't know what to think. For the life of him, he didn't know whether he'd hit the bird or not. But Mr. Green jumped up and yelled triumphantly as he ran toward the goose, flopping about in the water.

"You got us breakfast!" he shouted, as he drew the bird toward the shore with a stick. "I ain't tasted goose in a long spell. We'll eat it and save the grease."

Flan stared at the dead goose. The smooth feathers lay neatly over the breast and wings.

The red blood dripped slowly from the torn neck.

"It's a nice one," the Long Hunter went on. "And that was a fine shot."

A fine shot! Flan looked up. He'd shot this goose himself. He'd pulled the trigger and fired the ball and killed a goose. The first game he'd ever killed. And he hadn't even had to steady his rifle in a tree or over a log. He'd shot a goose, all by himself. He reached out and seized the bird by its black feet. There was a swirl of yellow hickory leaves as he ran back toward the fire.

"Mr. Rhea! Mr. Rhea!" he yelled. "I shot a goose! Down in the creek. I shot a goose, and I never steadied the rifle with nothing! I shot it all by myself and knocked its head clean off! Ain't it a fine one?"

Mr. Rhea took the bird and held it up. "It ain't got much fat on it," he said at last, after he'd punched it a time or two. "Young bird like that don't roast too well."

"It'll taste fine, just the same," said Mr.

Green. "We never stopped to ask her was she old and tough, did we, Flan?" and he winked at the boy.

It did taste fine, and Mr. Rhea cut off one of the wings and gave it to Flan to keep. Flan wished he could have saved the feathers for his mam. She saved every feather she could lay her hands on, to keep her feather beds full and fat. Some day she aimed to have feather pillows, she told Flan. When he was a lawyer and rich, he'd buy her feather pillows.

But maybe he thought, as they started up the trail and the sun shone down and the day began to warm, maybe he'd not be a lawyer. Maybe he'd be a great hunter. He'd come in after months in the woods, with his horses loaded with furs and skins, and he'd be rich enough to buy all the feather pillows in creation.

He grinned to himself. Here he'd shot one goose and he was off day-dreaming about how he was the world's finest hunter. He was a light-head and no mistake. It took a heap more than being a good shot to get along out in the woods.

119

Still it was a wonderful feeling, to have shot a goose and eaten it for breakfast. He whistled as he walked along the trace holding Meg's lead rope.

"I reckon all that cold water yesterday must of done the boy good," said Mr. Rhea. "I never seen him so cheerful."

"It's the sun makes me feel so good," answered Flan. "I . . . I could lick my weight in painters," he added and looked sheepish. When his brothers said that, they sounded tough and strong and big as all outdoors, but he didn't sound anything but foolish.

"You don't weigh but half a painter," pointed out Mr. Rhea.

"Which half'll you fight, Flan? The front half or the behind half?" asked Mr. Green.

"I'll fight the tail half of one that's got a head on both ends," said Flan after a minute. Even Mr. Rhea had to laugh.

"I'll tell you about one time I fought a catamount," Mr. Green said. "I shot me a turkey, and it fell out of a tree near a bluff and landed on a little ledge running along under the bluff. I aimed to have that turkey, for I'd spent the best part of a day chasing it.

"But that was a mighty little ledge of rock. I figured I'd leave my rifle up on the bluff, and then I could get down on the ledge and get my bird and shinny back, the Lord willing. So I did just that. I clumb down and reached for my turkey, and just then a big old painter reached for me.

"I started along that ledge, but it soon ended, and the painter kept on a-coming. I reached for my hunting knife and that varmint took it plumb out of my hand and throwed it over the cliff. It come on at me with its mouth wide open and showing every tooth in its head."

"Did you . . . did you jump?" asked Flan. He wondered what he'd do if he met a panther like that on a ledge of rock. Even if he had a rifle, he reckoned he'd be too scared to use it. He could almost see the great red mouth and the sharp glistening teeth coming at him.

"Well, he come closer and closer and opened

his mouth wider. I could see plumb down to the root of his tail. So quick as a wink I reached in and grabbed it. I gave one most powerful jerk and turned that painter inside out. Then I picked up my turkey and went on my way."

Flan laughed and Mr. Green chuckled, but Mr. Rhea said sourly, "There's been many a man had a catamount's claw marks left on him that don't think that's so funny. I heard tell of a boy about Flan's age got killed by one over on the Yadkin two winters ago."

Flan sobered. He'd heard tell of terrible things about panthers too. He wondered if they were true. He wondered if Mr. Green really had met one of the beasts on a ledge, and what he'd really done. Well, he'd never know. Mr. Green hardly ever told anything that actually happened to him, just one of those wild stories. Flan grinned. He'd a heap rather hear Mr. Green's wild tales than Mr. Rhea's sad ones.

They walked on. The next day they found evidence that a big party of settlers was ahead of them, and they hurried forward.

Flan kept up, though they went at a good pace. The trail led over low hills, and there were no more steep mountainsides to make his legs and his side ache, and no more rocky winding stretches. The sun shone and the forest was bright with red and yellow and orange. Beech leaves carpeted the ground and made a gold light among the trees. When Flan got a chance, he snatched up a handful of nuts to eat as he walked.

" 'Tain't far to Little Laurel River," said Mr. Green in the middle of the afternoon, and suddenly a man stepped out of the bushes up ahead.

"Howdy, strangers," the man said. "Where you headed for?"

Mr. Green stopped the horses and replied, "The French Lick. There's a party of folks up ahead and we figured to join up with 'em. You ain't seen 'em?"

The man nodded. "I be them."

Mr. Green laughed. "Smallest party of folks I ever seen."

The stranger grinned. "Well, I reckon I ain't

but one of 'em. I'm a-looking out for Injuns. You seen any signs of 'em?"

Mr. Green shook his head. "Not since Cumberland Gap."

"The folks I'm with ain't but a little piece up ahead," said the stranger and stepped back in the bushes.

"Come along," said Mr. Green and tugged at the horses.

Flan hurried after. Company! A whole party of folks! It was all he could do to keep from breaking loose and running up the trail.

Chapter Eight

FLAN AND MR. GREEN stood to one side as the trader knelt on the ground and spread his wares on a deerskin in front of him. The women crowded up close about him while the children peeped around their skirts and the men looked over their wives' shoulders.

Some one stepped on a dog's tail and it howled.

"Let me see, Mammy," one of the smaller children whimpered. Flan looked too. He'd never seen what the trader carried in his pack.

"I got ribbons, all color ribbons," said Mr. Rhea in a sing-song voice. "I got two yards of lace from across the seas. I got needles, I got pins." As he talked, he laid the articles down in little heaps. "I got scissors, I got knives, I got hatchets. Here's a looking glass, and here's combs. Thimbles and bullet molds. Something for each and every."

The women began to turn over the merchandise looking at everything, but Mr. Rhea was not through. Carefully he laid on the deerskin a pewter plate and a few pewter spoons. Then he brought out something wrapped in cloth and slowly began to undo it. The women watched eagerly.

"Ladies," spoke Mr. Rhea impressively, "this here is a silver spoon, a real solid silver spoon."

Flan pressed closer. There it lay on the trader's hands gleaming dully. It didn't look any different from the pewter spoons to him.

But he knew it was. Made of silver and fit to grace a king's table. He'd often heard his mam talk of the silver spoon her mother had had back in Virginny. Sometimes she told him when he was a rich lawyer, they'd have a heap of silver spoons.

Now the women began to bargain with the trader. They handled the silver spoon and admired the ribbons, but mostly they bought needles or other household goods. One man bought a bullet mold, saying he had lost his in the Cumberland River.

One woman stood near Flan and Mr. Green while her husband tried out hatchet after hatchet, looking for one that suited him. A boy and girl about Flan's age stood with her.

"Do ye aim to travel with us awhile?" she asked politely. "You're welcome to take victuals with us, such as it is. Cordell's our name."

"Thank ye kindly, ma'am," answered Mr. Green. "I reckon we'll go along with you for a spell. And if somebody's got a horse that can

127

carry the trader's pack and give my horse's back a chance to heal, I'd be mighty obliged."

The woman's husband turned toward them with his hatchet. "I seen them burns," he said. "How'd that happen?"

Flan looked at the burn on his hand and waited for Mr. Green to tell about the fire and how he'd saved the horses. He glanced toward the campfire where the women were making supper and tried to pretend he wasn't listening to Mr. Green. Several other men and boys had gathered around now to hear the story.

"Well, it was this-a-way," the Long Hunter began. "We was at the Cumberland Gap and started down the other side when all at once we seen a fire come sweeping up the mountainside straight at us. Flames as tall as the mountains and smoke as thick as muddy water. We started back the way we'd come up, but what should we see coming up the trail but a war party of Injuns, a whole passel of 'em. The fire was right up on us and the Injuns was coming fast."

Flan's mouth hung open in astonishment. He might have known Mr. Green wouldn't tell the truth. The others were listening breathlessly as though they believed every word of it.

"I sat down on a rock for I figured I'd come to the end of my days. I was going to let which ever got there first have me, the fire or the Injuns. But Flan here grabbed a burning pine tree and threw it at them Injuns and killed every ding one of 'em. And then he turned around and spit on that fire and put it out."

The men roared with laughter and the Cordell boy slapped his knee and laughed too. Flan wanted to keep his face solemn the way Mr. Green did, as if the story was the gospel truth, but he couldn't help grinning.

It was kind of disappointing not to be bragged about, but Mr. Green never boasted about what he'd done. Flan reckoned he wouldn't boast about what Flan had done either. It made him feel good to think that Mr. Green treated him like a real Long Hunter.

But he would have liked to tell that boy and

129

girl about how he had rescued the horses from burning, and about how he had rafted the swollen Cumberland River and nearly drowned.

He and Mr. Green went and sat by the campfire. Mr. Green cleaned his rifle and molded some bullets. He said he could smell Indians.

"Aye," Mr. Cordell answered. "We've seen signs of the savages and we got scouts out. We'll keep a good watch tonight."

Mrs. Cordell brought Flan a trencher heaped with deer meat and ashcake.

"There ain't no milk," she told him. "It's hard traveling without a cow. Some of the chaps is ailing and I know in reason they need milk. But I hear tell they have a heap of cows at Logan's Station. That's where we're headed."

Flan thanked her and ate his supper. He was so hungry it didn't matter what he had to eat, but it did seem like Mrs. Cordell's deer meat and ash cake tasted better than Mr. Rhea's.

He gazed around him. There were three families in the party, and some extra men, young men about as old as his brothers. One of them stopped and spoke to him. "You come all the way from the Blockhouse on foot?"

Flan nodded.

"You're a better walker than I am, then," the man remarked good-naturedly. "I'd of give out long ago."

He walked on and Mrs. Cordell's son took his trencher and sat by Flan.

He was a round-faced, sturdy-looking boy with blue eyes. "My name's Wiley Cordell," he told Flan.

"Mine's Flan Taylor," said Flan. He stabbed a piece of deer meat with his hunting knife.

"Is he your pappy?" asked Wiley, nodding at Mr. Green.

"Naw," answered Flan. "I'm just a-journeying with him." He hoped he looked like a boy who traveled through the wilderness all the time, falling in with anybody who chanced along.

"You got a knife," said Wiley. "Kind of new, ain't it?"

Flan didn't answer.

"Ain't you got a hatchet?"

Flan shook his head.

"Ain't you got a rifle?"

Flan opened his mouth to say no, he didn't have a rifle but he could shoot and only yesterday he'd shot a goose, when Wiley Cordell hurried on.

"I ain't got a rifle, but my pa lets me shoot his, and last week I shot a deer, a good big 'un. I aimed to tan the hide, but there ain't no way to do it whilst we're riding along."

Flan was glad he hadn't said anything about shooting that goose.

One of the dogs came nosing up to Wiley and he pushed it away. "How old be you?" Wiley asked next.

"Ten," mumbled Flan.

"I was eleven last week," said Wiley proudly. "My sister Nancy's almost ten. She can shoot too. But she's just a girl. And she ain't much good. She can't do none of the silly things girls is supposed to do. She can't cook or sew. You ought to see the mess she makes when she tries to spin. Ma says she can't even sweep the hearth without knocking the bedstead down."

Flan glanced toward the little girl with brown pigtails who was stirring the stew in a big pot over the fire. She smiled at him and he smiled shyly back. Here was another unhandy one. Maybe he'd tell her about the goose.

Mrs. Cordell came hurrying up. "Nancy! Mercy on us. You let it boil over. Here, give me the spoon. It's a sight easier to do things myself than clean up after you doing 'em!"

She seized the spoon, looking exasperated, and Nancy came to sit by her brother and Flan. She did not seem upset.

"Wooden-head!" jeered Wiley.

"I reckon so," she answered cheerfully. "I never wanted to stir the old stew anyway. I'm ding nigh roasted."

"Girls ain't supposed to swear," said Wiley.

"Boys ain't supposed to be so sassy," said Nancy, spreading her calico skirt around her and looking very prim and ladylike. "Be you going to Kentuck?"

Flan grinned at her and shook his head. "We're headed for the French Lick."

Wiley grunted and got up. Nancy laughed. "He don't like for me to hang around him," she told Flan. "He don't think I'm much good. My ma thinks I'm no account too. She says I'll never get a husband."

"I ain't much account neither," said Flan suddenly. "I don't know much about nothing. I'm only just learning to shoot. But I can shoot pretty good. I shot a goose yesterday."

"Well, I wish you'd shot it today," exclaimed Nancy. "I'm sick to death of deer meat. Look, yonder's Clarke Miller. He's going to get out his fiddle and we'll have us a jollification."

In the fading twilight the travelers gathered around the fire. The man took his fiddle from a deerskin poke and pressed it against his chest. To Flan the music sounded wonderful. It wasn't often in his life he'd heard a fiddle, and out here in the dark and the wilderness its squeaking tones sounded brave and sweet and gay.

First the fiddler scraped out a fast dance tune.

Several couples got up and danced, but it was rough going on the uneven ground, and some of the dancers did more jumping over bushes than they did hopping to the music.

Flan would have liked to dance. It looked like it might be fun to kick up your heels and go flying around to the thumping beat of the reels. But he'd hate to go the wrong way and go hopping when he should be skipping. Instead he beat time to the music with his foot.

One of the older boys danced by himself because there wasn't a girl for him to partner. He shouted and kicked and hopped and twirled. The fiddler sawed away faster and faster and everybody yelled encouragement to the dancer, who showed off more than ever. Flan and Nancy laughed aloud together.

The dance tune ceased and the dancers flung themselves panting on the ground. Flan looked around for Mr. Green, but he wasn't there. He reckoned the Long Hunter was out scouting for Indians. He stared off into the black night out-

side the circle of firelight. He was glad he was with folks.

The fiddler was talking. "Now some folks say that the fiddle belongs to the devil and anybody who plays dance tunes on a fiddle is headed straight for Old Scratch. Well, I ain't a-knowing. But if the devil comes after me, here's a song I learned that'll keep him off me—I hope." He grinned at them.

Then he played and sang a song about a girl who had to answer nine riddles the devil asked her, or lose her soul. Flan thought she must be a right quick girl, for she answered all nine right off, quick as a wink. He was glad she didn't have to go to the devil.

"Aw, I know a better riddle than them," sang out Wiley Cordell as the music stopped. "I reckon none of you all will know this one."

"Wiley always thinks he's smarter than other folks," said Nancy to Flan. "The answer to his old riddle will be a egg. You watch and see. It always is."

"A long white barn,
Two roofs on it,
And no door at all, at all,"

said Wiley solemnly.

He looked around for a second or two, and then, fearful that someone would answer, he shouted out, "A egg! A egg!"

Everybody laughed and Nancy giggled and punched Flan. "I told you," she whispered.

Now the fiddler played and sang a funny tune or two. Then he sang *Barbara Ellen*, that Flan knew, and finally the one about the golden ball and the maid that was going to be hanged. That was one Flan's mam liked to sing. It seemed like he could almost hear her singing as she stirred the soap kettle in the yard at home, or churned out under the trees. Mam always sang when she churned. And when she had fresh butter she always made a cobbler if there were berries to be had. He wished he could see her now. He wished he could see his brothers and his pap and his sister, Rosedel.

The travelers were getting ready for bed now. The mothers were getting the children into the blankets and the men were deciding who would stand guard. Flan wondered where his mother was that night, and if she was thinking of him.

He got out his blanket and spread it on some brush heaped up for a bed. Mr. Rhea was talking to someone. Flan could hear their voices.

"Aye, he's taking the powder casks and the boy to the French Lick," the trader said.

"They'll be glad to get the powder, if there's anybody left alive there," the other answered. "I've heard tell the Injuns has well nigh wiped out the settlements at Nashborough."

Flan crouched by his bed. Was it true? Was his mam not thinking of him because she lay dead in the forest somewhere? And his pap and all his big black-haired brothers? Was he all alone in the world?

He crept into his bed and lay there wretchedly, staring up into the night sky. Would he never see any of them again?

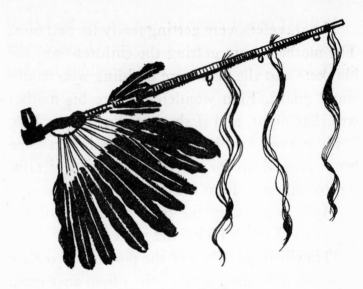

Chapter Nine

ONCE IN THE NIGHT Flan heard the men who had been on guard outside the camp come in and wake the men who were to take their places. He raised his head and saw Chapman Green standing by the low fire.

When he awoke the next morning he looked around again for Mr. Green, but he couldn't find him. He tied up his bedding and put it near the trader's pack.

Wiley Cordell came by, lugging a bucket of water. "Come on," he told Flan. "I got to get some wood. You get that trader feller's hatchet and come with me."

Flan hesitated. He didn't want to chop wood, but he wanted to go with Wiley. The trader's ax lay across his pack. Finally Flan picked it up and walked over to the fire where Wiley was talking to his mother and sister.

Mrs. Cordell took the piggin of water. "Now, Wiley, don't go far. You can get enough wood without running clean back to Cumberland Gap." She turned back to the fire. "Nancy! For the Lord's mercy! Watch that dough! It's all running out in the ashes!"

She snatched up the ash board and began to scrape the dough off it. "Git the baby and mind him. Don't let him fall in the creek. If'n there was just one thing you could do right!"

Nancy swung the baby up on her hip and as the two boys started off she followed behind.

"Go on back," Wiley ordered. "We don't want you a-tagging on after us."

"Make me," said Nancy calmly.

Wiley turned red in the face, but he looked as though he had tried to make his sister do things before this and failed. He walked on, swinging his ax fiercely. They followed the creek for a short distance and then came to a place where several small trees had been felled by a larger tree falling across them.

"Here," said Wiley. "That's good dry wood. Ma'll like that."

He set to work with his hatchet and Flan selected another tree and began to work too. He swung the ax up and down in short strokes, but he didn't seem to be doing much good. A heap of splinters flew about, but nothing came of it.

Wiley stopped and looked at him. "You ain't much hand at chopping," he commented at last. Flan pressed his lips together and didn't answer.

"You ain't got a-hold of it right, for one thing," Wiley went on. "Grab the handle down at the end and you'll do better."

Flan flushed. "I can chop to suit me," he said

angrily and pulled his hand away from the other boy's. Wiley shrugged and went back to his chopping. Flan stood holding his hatchet and wishing he hadn't come. Nancy sat in a loop of grapevines, holding the baby and swinging gently.

"I mind when Wiley first started doing the chopping," said Nancy dreamily. "Pa said for Wiley to be careful, and Wiley said he would. First day he hit his toes and liked to chopped 'em off of one foot, and next day he well nigh chopped 'em off the other foot. He had to stay a-bed for a whole week." She giggled and Flan grinned a little. Wiley just went on chopping.

Flan remembered how he hadn't wanted to learn to shoot, how he'd put his hands behind him when Mr. Green tried to make him take the gun. What a muddle-head he was! Here he was trying not to find out the right way to chop. A body had to learn from somebody. It was better to chop off your toes, than always to be worrying about doing the wrong thing and never learning at all.

He watched Wiley a minute. Wiley raised the ax in his right hand and brought it down in a smooth curve. Finally Flan went up close to Wiley and mumbled, "I shouldn't ought to have been so hasty. Show me how to hold it."

Wiley stood up. "Grab the handle way down at the end and take a full swing with it like this." He swung his own ax up and down while Flan watched. He kept on chopping steadily, cutting the small tree trunks into lengths and then standing these on end and splitting them lengthwise.

Flan turned back to his own tree. He tried to follow Wiley's instructions and sure enough he did better. He couldn't often hit twice in the same place but the hatchet bit into the wood with a satisfying ring. He didn't work very fast, but he did get his tree cut into lengths. He was glad he'd listened to what Wiley told him.

Nancy swung and sang to the baby. A woodpecker drummed overhead. Flan chopped and chopped. He looked up suddenly to see Chapman Green coming toward him.

"You young 'uns are a good piece from camp," Mr. Green said worriedly. "There's Injuns about. You got no call to stray so far." He looked at the firewood and grinned. "You got enough wood for two fires, ain't you?"

Flan and Wiley gathered up the wood. There was quite a heap of it. They had to leave some behind. The Long Hunter didn't carry any. He kept his hands free so he could use his rifle, if he saw a deer, he said. Flan wondered if he meant Indian instead of deer.

After breakfast Mr. Cordell told them to hurry and pack their belongings. Flan watched. It was good to see folks stirring around thick as flies in August. The men helped the women onto the horses and handed the least ones up to them. One woman carried a rifle across her lap while a little girl sat behind her and held onto her. All the horses carried other things besides the women and children—bundles, pots and pans, and wallets of food.

Nancy told Flan that she and Wiley took turns riding an old mare named Brink. Some-

145

times they rode together, but her pa didn't like to have them both on the horse for long distances. They moved off single file along the trail, and Flan fell in with them, feeling strange to be setting out with so many people.

Mrs. Cordell rode up beside Flan. "Your ma won't know you when you get to the French Lick," she told him. "It changes a young 'un a heap to make a long journey a-foot. I don't know why, but it seems like it's always so."

Flan thought this over solemnly. He reckoned he had changed a heap. He wasn't so unhandy as he used to be. And he didn't mind it so much when folks laughed at his awkwardness. He reckoned he'd just never got it through his head that folks had to start learning things somewhere. Maybe it took him a little longer than most folks, maybe there'd always be things he wasn't too good at. But he wasn't as slow-witted as his brothers made out, he knew that now for a fact.

One of the other women spoke up. "I'm glad

it wasn't my boy had to come over that trail with a half-wild hunter."

"Mr. Green ain't wild," Flan said quickly. "He's a fine man. He's took good care of me." He glared at the woman.

"Well," she answered with a sniff, "he ain't let the Injuns get you yet. But it's easy seen he let you get mixed up with a fire someway. You got a burn on your hand and your shirt's scorched. And you don't look like you been eating too good."

Flan glanced ahead to see if Mr. Green had heard any of this. But he was way up ahead talking to one of the scouts.

He let the woman ride on. It made him mad to have that woman talk that way about as good and kind a man as Chapman Green. And he reckoned if Indians attacked them, she'd be glad to have a Long Hunter along. Uncle Henry had told Flan that Mr. Green was a famous Indian fighter.

"Don't pay her no mind," muttered Wiley. "She talks that way about everybody."

They walked on in silence and then Wiley asked, "How did you get burned like that?"

Flan hesitated. He didn't know how to make up a wild tale like Mr. Green's. Finally he told Wiley what had happened. He tried not to boast about it, but it was hard not to show this other boy that he could be brave and act quickly when he had to.

Wiley looked at him admiringly. "I wish it was me going with Mr. Green," he said. "It sure is slow poking along with all these chaps and the womenfolks. I wouldn't mind walking."

Flan thought that Wiley might not mind walking, but he wasn't very good at it. Flan was glad to find that he was better at something than Wiley was. The older boy kept running ahead and lagging behind, stepping off the trail to see things and then having to hurry to catch up. He didn't keep walking at a steady even pace, and by noon he was red-faced and panting.

"I reckon I'll let Nancy walk a little while," he told Flan finally. "It'll be good for her, she's so lazy."

Nancy dismounted and Wiley climbed up on Brink. Flan grinned at the little girl. "I reckon you've done more walking than Wiley on this journey," he said.

Nancy giggled. "I don't mind. I'd a heap rather walk than ride on that bony old Brink. She's most too old to come such a ways anyhow. And Ma always ties the skillet on her and it bumps my legs when I ride."

Once Mr. Cordell urged Flan to ride, but he shook his head. He was used to walking now, riding might make him sore again. And he didn't get tired when he had so much company.

They traveled three days with the Kentucky bound party. In the evenings Wiley helped Flan scrape out the inside of the horn Mr. Green had given him for a cup, and one of the scouts fitted the big end of it with a piece of hickory and made a stopper for the other. Flan felt proud of his powder horn, only he wished he had a rifle to go with it.

In the afternoon of the third day Mr. Green called Flan to him. "We need fresh meat bad,"

149

he told the boy. "Let's you and me strike out and see can we get us a deer. I told Cordell we'd meet him at the head of Dick's River along about sundown."

As they set off away from the others Flan turned and waved at the Cordell children. Nancy waved back, but Wiley stuck out his tongue. Flan laughed. He knew Wiley wanted to go hunting with a real Long Hunter too.

Mr. Green said, "We'll hit across here to the creek and follow it down till it joins up with another to make Dick's River."

The Long Hunter turned and started off through the trees at a trot. It wasn't long till they reached the creek and turned downstream. There were plenty of canebrakes along the flat land so they traveled mostly back among the trees to avoid the brakes. It seemed to Flan they went a long way through the woods without seeing any sign of game. But he liked being off the trail for a while.

Just then they heard something crashing

through the woods and coming toward them. Mr. Green pulled Flan to one side behind some laurel bushes. Three does followed by a buck broke across a clearing right beside where they lay. The Long Hunter raised his rifle, but he didn't shoot. Flan looked around at him in surprise.

Mr. Green was peering through the trees before them. He leaned over and whispered in the boy's ear. "Something scared them deer. You follow me close and step right where I step. And don't make a sound."

There was something sharp and urgent in the hunter's voice that made Flan keep quiet and not ask any questions. When the hunter began to crawl toward a beech tree, Flan was right on his heels. The sun was low in the west and Flan wished they'd hurry and join the others. He crept forward keeping his eyes on the ground.

There was a touch on his shoulder and he looked up quickly. Mr. Green motioned him up beside him. They were behind a small outcrop-

ping of rocks. Flan looked cautiously through the bushes to where the hunter pointed, and what he saw made him turn cold from head to foot.

Three Indians lay hidden in the grass, watch-

ing the Cordell's making camp. And as Flan
watched, he saw several more shadowy forms
move off to one side as though to surround the
camp.

Indians—between them and the camp!

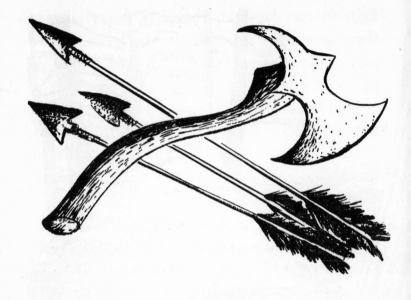

Chapter Ten

SILENTLY, SLOWLY, Chapman Green drew Flan back and back among the trees. The man's eyes darted to every tree and bush. At last he stopped and looked all around very carefully. Then he began to speak in a hurried whisper.

"Now listen, Flan, and listen careful, for we ain't got much time. Them Injuns is waiting for dark to attack the camp. They won't try to fight in the daylight, they like everything in their favor. We got to warn the folks if'n we aim to save all our scalps. And you got to do it."

Flan looked up startled. The Long Hunter began to pick up a few rocks from the ground.

"I reckon he's daft," thought Flan. "If'n he figures I'm going to fling rocks at them savages, I *know* he's daft."

"Hold out your shirt tail," whispered Mr. Green and Flan obeyed. Mr. Green put the rocks in the sack Flan made by holding up the long tail of his hunting shirt. The hunter began to speak rapidly.

"Now them Injuns won't want to give theirselves away. They'll lay quiet till after dark as long as nobody sees 'em. What you got to do is walk to the camp like you had a shirt tail full of persimmons . . ." He broke off, looking around. "No, them little winter grapes'll do." He moved over to a vine and began to strip the little blue fruits from it and scatter them over the rocks in Flan's shirt tail.

"Now you walk on to the camp, slow and easy, like there wasn't an Injun between here and the ocean. They'll never risk giving an alarm for the chance at your scalp, as long as you make out like you don't know they're there. But you mustn't run. You mustn't look scared. Walk along slow and eat some of them grapes. When you get to the camp, you go straight up to Mr. Cordell and act like you was giving him some grapes. Tell him not to let on, but to get the womenfolks and the tads down in the cane by the creek as quick as he can. I'll give you time enough for that, and then I'll fire. We won't wait till them red devils want to fight, we'll fight now and surprise them. Do you understand?"

Flan nodded. "Can't you come with me?" he whispered hoarsely.

Mr. Green grinned. "Naw, them Injuns would know something was wrong if'n they saw me out here picking grapes. Besides I'm more use back here behind them. I can kill me at least one Injun afore they know we've started fighting."

Flan still stood. "I can't," he said at last.

Mr. Green took him firmly by the shoulder. He looked down at him a minute. "You got to," he said simply and gave the boy a little shove.

Once he began to move, Flan kept going, although he wanted desperately to turn back. His heart was thumping loudly, his knees felt so stiff he could hardly bend them. His feet went forward without him having anything to do with them, it seemed to him. Once he stumbled and nearly dropped his shirt tail full of rocks and grapes. It scared him half to death.

His face felt tight and swollen, like once when a lot of bees had stung him. He came to a heavy clump of bushes and he paused. For a moment he thought he could not make himself go forward past the undergrowth. He looked up and through the trees ahead he saw the campfire. He could even see folks moving about the fire. It was a long way off, but the sight of friends gave him courage.

157

On he walked past the bushes with his heart racing, glancing out of the corner of his eyes, half expecting to see a brown arm reach for him. Whose eyes were watching him from behind every tree? He scuffed the dry leaves as he walked, so that all the Indians would know he was coming and have time to hide.

He walked and walked, and yet the camp didn't seem to come any closer. He kept staring at the ground, then glancing up expectantly after he'd gone miles, it felt like, but the fire was still just as far away.

Something slid around a tree to one side. Flan stared ahead trying not to look. A rock lying by a bush slowly drew itself back among the undergrowth, and Flan realized the rock had been a foot. His scalp tightened on his head and the sweat ran down his face.

The trees thinned as he came toward the head of Dick's River. Hope sprang up in him. He had reckoned he'd go on walking for days among the savages, never getting any nearer the camp, like a walk in a nightmare.

He hoped he was walking along naturally. Surely he was moving too slow. He speeded up in a panic, and then he thought he was going too fast. He looked down to take some grapes to eat and found he had squeezed a handful without knowing it. The red sticky juice stained his fingers and shirt. He threw the pulp away and tried to eat a grape, but his throat was so tight and dry he could not swallow.

But suddenly he was right up on the camp. His heart leaped. He was going to make it. He wasn't going to be tomahawked from behind and silently scalped. He was going to get back to the camp and warn Mr. Cordell and save the party. He wanted to run, but he didn't. He kept on as slowly and calmly as he could. He hoped Wiley or Nancy didn't run out to meet him. They'd sure let on something was the matter if they saw him carrying those stones along with the grapes.

At last, there he was, near the campfire. He drew a deep breath of relief. And then he realized that he was not yet safe, that he must warn the others and get ready for the Indian attack. Walking through the woods had been only a beginning to the danger.

Wiley came toward him. "What you got in your shirt, a bear?" he asked jeeringly. "I knew you wouldn't shoot nothing."

Mr. Cordell turned from the fire. "Where's Green?" he asked sharply. "What's the matter?"

Flan held up his shirt tail.

"Take some of them grapes," he said in a voice that he tried to keep from sounding high and shrill with fright. He was shaking a little bit. "Act like you wanted everybody to have some. There's Injuns all around the camp, and Mr. Green says they're waiting for dark. He says get the women and young 'uns down by the creek in the cane. Only don't let on you know about the Injuns. Act like you always do. When Mr. Green fires that'll be the signal to go out after the Injuns and not wait for them to start the fight."

Mr. Cordell turned and called out to his wife.

"Selina, come have some of these here little fox grapes."

Mrs. Cordell handed Nancy the spoon with which she was stirring the stew. She came up smiling and took a grape from Flan's shirt.

Flan had to admire her for she never blinked an eye when she saw the rocks in there with the grapes, nor when Mr. Cordell told her of the Indians. Several of the other adults gathered around to hear, and in a few minutes everyone in camp knew the Indians were waiting to attack.

But nobody ran or hollered or seemed frightened. One by one the women and younger children slipped away down toward the creek. Flan wished they'd hurry a little because the sun was slipping down the sky. It was already dim, back among the trees.

"Wiley, you and Flan stay here," ordered Mr. Cordell. "It'll look bad if all the young 'uns leave. As soon as you hear the shot, you get down in the cane with the others, you hear? And some of you boys watch the horses."

Flan and Wiley nodded. One of the older

161

girls stayed too, stirring the stew just as though she were getting ready to call them to supper.

"I'll keep an eye on this powder of Green's," Mr. Rhea volunteered.

Wiley whispered to Flan, "You mean you just walked right through them Injuns and come on into camp?"

Flan nodded and just then the shot rang out. From the woods came a wild blood-chilling war whoop that made him go weak all over. Mr. Cordell shouted an order, the dogs barked and yelped furiously, and the girl by the fire dropped the spoon and fled through the trees toward the creek.

Flan stood still a minute, while the men ran by him. "Git down, young 'uns," someone shouted.

Flan turned to go down to the canebrake, but Wiley was crouching behind a log among some calico bushes, and Flan followed. He was shivering a little with excitement, but he was glad he wasn't down in the brake. They could see the whole fight from here. He looked carefully over the log and at first he couldn't see anything except Mr. Cordell crouched behind a tree.

The dogs ran forward baying, their yelps growing louder as they surrounded a tree. A dark figure stepped from behind it swinging a tomahawk frantically at the leaping dogs. One dog ran howling into the woods, another sank to the ground. The others fell back snarling.

Mr. Cordell fired his rifle. The dark figure dropped to the ground and the yelping dogs sprang at it. There were more shots and figures moved from tree to tree, but Flan could not always make out whether it was Indians or not. Wiley kept wriggling restlessly beside him and saying over and over that he wished he had him a rifle, he'd show those redskins.

Suddenly a figure came running through the woods. There was no mistaking the Long Hunter. He dodged from tree to tree like a shadow, but he didn't seem to be in a hurry. He looked like a man who knew well enough what he was doing.

"Cordell!" shouted Mr. Green. "Get somebody down by the creek. There's two of them devils a-sneaking along the bank toward the womenfolks! The rest watch them horses! Most of the Injuns is over there."

He disappeared behind a bush and fired at the same time. Flan watched him pour in powder as he moved forward to the shelter of a tree, never pausing as he rammed the lead ball down the barrel and left the tree for a patch of cane near the horses. Flan marveled that the hunter loaded his rifle without once looking down to see where he was going, but always watching the woods around him as he moved ahead. Mr. Green was a real Injun fighter. Flan was proud of him. He hoped that woman who had called the hunter "wild" was seeing this.

The horses whinnied in terror at the sounds of the steady firing around them. They thrashed about in the cane, milling against each other. Flan could see three or four of them stumbling about on the rough ground with their hobbled feet.

Suddenly two Indians ran forward and at-

164

tempted to cut the hobbles. At once Chapman Green appeared from nowhere and struck one of the Indians across the head with his tomahawk. The other savage turned and grappled with the Long Hunter, grabbing his upraised right arm.

They fought among the frightened animals, swaying first this way and that. The hunter couldn't free his arm from the red man's grasp to use his tomahawk. Flan started up out of the bushes, clenching his fists in fear for Mr. Green.

Chapman Green sent his left fist crashing into the side of the Indian's face, at the same time twisting his right arm free from the other's grip, and hitting the Indian with the flat of his tomahawk. The savage fell back under the pawing hoofs of the horses and Flan sank down behind the log.

Mr. Green moved back to the shadows of the trees to aid one of the white men who was backed up against a tree swinging his broken rifle at an Indian who waited an opportunity to rush him with a knife. The Indian faded back at the approach of the hunter, but Mr. Green pursued him around some bushes and out of Flan's range of vision.

There was a rustle in the undergrowth behind the two boys. Wiley looked at Flan with frightened eyes. Was it an Indian creeping toward them? They pressed up close to the log, hoping not to be noticed.

Beyond them one of the Indians crawled on his hands and knees. He had not seen the boys yet. Flan held his breath. He remembered what Mr. Green had said about being small enough to hide from Indians and he hoped the calico bushes hid him. Finally when nothing happened, Wiley whispered, "Where . . . where did that 'un go?"

Flan peeped cautiously over the log and saw that the Indian was creeping up behind the trader. Mr. Rhea was squatting near where the two powder casks were hidden and Flan reckoned he'd been there the whole time. The Indian stopped and slowly drew his feet up under him to spring.

Flan stood up and shouted, "Look out behind you, Mr. Rhea! Look out!"

Mr. Rhea turned quickly around, but he wasn't quick enough. The red man was on him and knocked the trader's gun from his hands as he turned. Mr. Rhea grabbed him and they began to sway back and forth on their feet. The savage was heavier and taller and he was slick with grease and paint. Mr. Rhea was having trouble holding him.

Suddenly the Indian wrenched his right arm free and gave a swing at the white man with his tomahawk. Mr. Rhea ducked the blow and jumped for his rifle, but the Indian pulled him away from it and they rolled to the ground with the red man on top. The Indian tried furiously to use his tomahawk, but the trader held onto the other's right hand, preventing him from using the weapon. They rolled and grunted among the dead leaves. Flan could see that the trader was weakening.

Suddenly Mr. Rhea's grip slipped from the other's wrist and the Indian lashed out with

the tomahawk. The trader squirmed aside but the blade bit into his shoulder.

"He's got the trader now," Wiley whispered hoarsely.

Flan looked around for help but he could see no one. Mr. Rhea was thrashing and wriggling about for all he was worth, but Flan knew he had better act now or it would be too late. He sprang toward the fallen rifle and picked it up. He hoped the powder hadn't been knocked from the pan.

He stuck out the gun, fingering the trigger, but the two men were moving about so he was afraid he would shoot Mr. Rhea.

He would have to get up closer. He came forward until the end of the gun all but touched the bronze back. For a moment he hesitated, half afraid to pull the trigger. Once more the Indian raised the tomahawk and as he did so, Flan fired.

The tomahawk fell to the ground and the Indian slumped forward half covering the trader's body with his own. Mr. Rhea lay so still that for a moment Flan was afraid he had killed him too. But then the white man struggled out from underneath the Indian and sat up.

Blood from the wound on his shoulder streamed down his arm. A pool of blood from the Indian's shattered head spread out toward Flan's mocassins and he moved back. He'd never seen so much blood. The woods reeled around him.

He held the gun out to the trader. "I never meant to use your gun without asking," he stammered.

Mr. Rhea, holding his hand to his wounded shoulder, looked up and smiled. "I'm glad you never waited to ask. I wouldn't a-been able to answer." He shook his head wearily and said, "Git back out of sight. There's Injuns around yet."

Once more Flan crouched behind the log with Wiley. "I killed an Injun," he said proudly.

Wiley jeered, "Shoot an Injun that close, you bound to kill him."

Flan didn't answer. He knew the older boy was jealous. A few random shots and shouts sounded through the woods, and then Mr. Cordell came walking toward them. One of the young men ran up from the creek and Mr. Cordell asked him, "The womenfolks all safe?"

The man nodded and Mr. Green appeared among the trees at the other side of the camp. "Cordell, we got the red devils on the run. I'll trail 'em aways to make sure they keep on going. You'd best get out some guards for the rest of the night." Then he was gone into the dark.

Wiley jumped up and ran to his father. "Pa, Flan shot an Injun. He saved that trader feller's life. Pa, do you hear?"

One of the women was dressing Mr. Rhea's wounded shoulder. "It's the gospel truth," the trader spoke up. "If it hadn't a-been for Flan, I'd be fit for nothing but the buzzards."

He told how Flan had shot the Indian and saved his life and all the womenfolks exclaimed over him. But Flan ate his stew and stared into the fire.

It was fine to have been brave and to have shot an Indian and to be praised for it. But he hoped he wouldn't ever have to do anything like that again. He'd just as soon forget this whole day and all its troubles.

Chapter Eleven

Nobody slept well that night and they were all up early. Mr. Cordell's party did not have much further to travel and they were anxious to get on to their destination.

"I couldn't abide another night in the open," said the woman who had called Mr. Green "wild."

Flan looked doleful. He knew that he and

Mr. Green had a good many more nights to spend in the open. Mr. Green had told him if everything went well, they'd reach the French Lick in two weeks. But it might be longer. Anyway he'd be getting nearer his folks every day.

Mr. Green had come into camp early that morning and told Mr. Cordell that there was no further danger from the Indians. "They're running yet, we whupped 'em so bad," he said.

Mr. Cordell nodded his head gravely. "Maybe so. But I'm worried about you and the boy setting out over the Barrens alone."

One of the younger men spoke up. " 'Tain't no need to worry. Them's two famous Injun fighters. I reckon Mr. Green ain't heard how Flan saved the trader's life."

When Chapman Green had heard the story he laughed and slapped Flan on the back. "If you ain't a ring-tail roarer! Didn't that redskin have a gun? Don't the lad get nothing for killing him an Injun?"

Mr. Cordell said, "Aye. We owe him something for warning us yesterday too. See which one of them rifles is the best and give it to him."

The Long Hunter carefully inspected the three rifles captured from the Indians. "This here is a pretty good one. Injuns don't know much how to take care of a rifle, but this 'un is in pretty good shape." He handed it to Flan.

Wiley spoke up and asked, "Can't I have one of them other rifles, Pa? Can't I?"

Mr. Cordell frowned. "Next Injun fight we're in, you get down in the canebrake like I tell you. Maybe you'll get a rifle then."

"It was sure lucky for me they weren't down in the cane," Mr. Rhea declared.

Flan reached out and took the gun. A rifle of his own! He wished he could show it to his brothers. He lifted the gun and sighted out through the trees.

"You'll need all the rifles you can lay your hands on when you cross the Barrens. There's Injuns and snakes and catamounts and sinkholes and every kind of a bad thing out there. Many a good man has met his end in the Barrens," Mr. Rhea stated discouragingly.

Chapman Green winked at Flan. "I'm sorry you ain't going to be with us, Rhea."

Mr. Rhea was going on with the others to Logan's Station. "Flan," said the trader, "before we part, I aim to let you have your pick of my wares for saving my skin."

He spread out the contents of his pack in front of Flan's eyes. "These are mighty fine hatchets, lad. Or maybe you'd like another knife." He held up the items as he talked. "You need a bullet mold with that new rifle."

Flan stood looking undecided. He knew what he wanted, but did he dare ask for it?

"Flan wants some of them red ribbons," teased Wiley.

"These are pretty good hatchets," Mr. Rhea repeated.

"I want the silver spoon," Flan blurted out.

The trader's mouth fell open. For a moment he looked a little sour. "Hit's worth the rest of my pack put together," he said. Then he laughed. "But I reckon if it hadn't been for you my pack wouldn't be worth anything a-tall to me now. Here's the spoon. I wish you luck of it."

Wiley stared at Flan. "You're addled in the head. I'd of took one of them hatchets."

"First time you kill an Injun, you take a hatchet," Nancy told her brother tartly, and he stuck his tongue out at her.

Although Wiley and the young men kidded him about his spoon, Flan only grinned and went on. The party moved off down the trail. Flan walked with Wiley and Nancy. He hated to think this was his last day with them. He liked being with all these friendly folks and he didn't look forward to the long lonely journey to the Lick.

A little beyond Whitley's Station the trail to the French Salt Lick turned off the Wilderness Trail. All the Cordell party gathered to tell Flan and Mr. Green good-bye and wish them luck.

Flan stood and watched the party disappear around a bend in the trail. Nancy Cordell, rid-

ing old Brink, was the last in the long line. Flan could see the skillet bumping against her leg as she rode. At the curve she turned and waved and he wondered if he would ever see her again.

For several days Flan and Mr. Green walked on through the forest. They crossed a heap of

small creeks, most of them choked with leaves.
Every little breeze sent the leaves whirling from
the trees. One night there was a wind that roared
and whistled all night long, and the next day
the trees were almost bare. Flan thought the
naked trees were ugly and gloomy looking, and
he was glad when they came to an oak forest,

where the great trees still kept most of their leaves.

The sun shone, and Mr. Green said they were making good time. But their good luck ran out when they forded the Little Barren River. Flan dropped his rifle in the water and they had to stop while they cleaned it and greased it with some of the goose grease the Long Hunter had saved.

While they worked, the horses strayed off down the river eating cane, and it took some little time to find them and bring them back to the trail.

After they passed the river, the country was different, Flan had never seen anything like it. As far as he could see in front of them, the land lay almost flat. There were no trees except on little knobby hills sticking up here and there. There were no rivers or creeks, but sometimes they passed deep sinkholes, and way at the bottom would be a tiny spring. Occasionally there were caves.

The ground was covered with long grass and

a dense tangle of briers and bushes. Mr. Green cautioned Flan to keep a sharp lookout for Indians. "That grass and stuff can hide a whole passel of Injuns. And they ain't above setting the grass a-fire and burning us up. It's been done often enough afore this."

Flan gazed all around. You could see for miles. It would be easy for Indians to watch them from the underbrush as they crossed the plain. Away off to the south he could see something dark moving along.

"What's that?" he asked, pointing.

"Buffalo," Mr. Green answered. "Not much of a herd."

Flan wished the Long Hunter would shoot one of the beasts. He'd always wanted to eat buffalo. Maybe when he got to Nashborough one of his brothers would shoot one. Or maybe—he remembered his rifle—maybe he'd shoot one himself. For a few minutes he walked along swinging his rifle and forgot about Indians.

The wind began to blow sharply under a cloudy sky, and soon the rain fell in a cold drizzle. Flan hunched his shoulders and pulled his shirt close around his neck, but the water trickled down his ears and neck and ran in rivulets down his back.

"Well, anyway," Mr. Green called good-naturedly over his shoulder, "we don't have to worry about fire." But Flan found this poor comfort. Now they made slow progress on the muddy, slippery trail.

One night while they were sleeping in a cave so low Flan couldn't stand up in it, there was a terrible sound from outside. Flan sat up, frightened half out of his wits. He'd never heard anything make a noise like that terrible screaming cry. Not the Indian war whoop nor the long wail of wolves they'd heard back in the mountains occasionally was as scarifying as this.

The horses whinnied in terror. Chapman Green sprang out of his blanket, reaching for his rifle. He smacked his head on the low ceiling of the cave. With a groan he rolled to the floor.

"It's a catamount, Flan," he moaned, scrambling up. "It's after the horses. Let's get out there and keep it off 'em."

Flan grabbed his own rifle and they ran outside. The rain had stopped but they couldn't see much in the cloudy night. The horses stirred restlessly and tossed their heads. The catamount must be lying in the long grass.

Flan clutched his rifle and listened. Mr. Green searched cautiously around the cave. "I reckon he smelled us and got scared off." He rubbed his head and then began to laugh. "The varmint sure gave me a lump on my head though."

Flan laughed too. Then they both went back to bed and to sleep, and nothing bothered them again that night.

They reached the Big Barren River. "The worst is over, Flan," said Chapman Green. "Maybe our luck will change when we leave the Barrens."

Flan hoped so. He didn't like the Barrens. He liked trees and mountains around a body, not this flat treeless land where an Injun could spy you three miles off.

Crossing the river Mr. Green stepped into a hole over his head. He came up spluttering and gasping, and mad as a wet hen. His coonskin cap had been swept off his head and lost in the river.

"First chance I get, I'll shoot you a new one," Flan told him consolingly.

"That one I had was nearly new, not more'n ten year old," said the Long Hunter disgustedly.

They went on, and soon they were back in the forested hills. Flan drew a deep breath of relief. They hadn't traveled through the woods more than half a day before he shot a deer. Mr. Green skinned it and cut up the meat.

"Next one I shoot, I'll skin myself," Flan boasted.

Mr. Green grinned. "I mind the first time I skinned a deer," he said. "Feller I was with said it looked like I didn't know which I was skinning, me or the deer."

But that night Mr. Green didn't eat any of the deer meat for supper. He fixed himself some tea and drank that, and he kept the fire going all night and slept right beside it.

184

The next day he was quiet, like he was thinking about something. Flan thought he'd never seen him walk so slow. And when they stopped at noon, he could see the Long Hunter shivering inside his buckskin shirt.

The next morning for the first time, Flan was up before the hunter. When Mr. Green sat up finally, Flan could see his face was flushed and feverish and he shivered and shook so he could hardly roll up his blanket.

"I got the ague bad," he told Flan. "It was going without my hat did it." Flan looked at him anxiously. "You use dogwood bark for the ague, my mam says," was all he could think to say.

"That's right," the hunter nodded. "I put some in my tea." He laughed a little. "Ain't it funny now? All the way over here we worried about you getting the shakes, and here it is me that's come down with 'em."

But Flan didn't think it was funny. Mr. Green looked like a pretty sick man. A spasm of shaking made him lean against a tree. He'd never be able to travel.

"It ain't but a little piece to the Lick," Mr. Green went on. "Not a day's journey. And no sign of Injuns. We'll make it all right."

They set out, but they went slower and slower. Mr. Green walked holding onto Meg's mane, stumbling and nearly falling every few steps. When the spells of shaking took him he let the horse half drag him over the rough trail. The sweat poured off him.

After an hour or so, he called to Flan. "I hate to do it, lad, but I got to stop," he gasped. He closed his eyes and leaned against the horse and shook till Flan thought he'd fall to the ground.

Finally he looked up again. "I know a hollow tree near here where I can go and hole up. You take the powder and go on. You'll be there long before sunset. You got a rifle and you can have plenty of powder and all them lead balls we molded back yonder." He wet his dry lips. "You'll be all right. Tell somebody to come after me with a riding horse."

Flan swallowed hard. There wasn't anything else to do, he could see that. Mr. Green might have the shakes for a week. And he needed somebody to nurse him. And the folks at the Lick needed the powder.

But he kept waiting for a chance to tell the hunter he couldn't do it. He didn't see how a ten-year-old boy could do it alone.

He helped Mr. Green through the woods to the hollow sycamore and spread out the blanket for him. Then he went back to the horses. He took hold of the lead thong and stared down the trail.

"Come along, Meg," he murmured, and gave the horse a little tug.

Chapter Twelve

FLAN STARTED along the trail, going slowly and carefully. He peered this way and that, trying to see around big trees or clumps of evergreen bushes. When he came to the top of a little rise, he stood there anxiously surveying the forest.

At last he started down. He was glad now that the leaves were mostly gone from the trees and underbrush. At least a body could see further than two feet on either side of the trail.

The horses clopped along behind him, blowing noisily and snatching at the bushes. He wished they'd be quieter. He rounded a curve cautiously. A woodpecker hammered loudly overhead and he jumped.

He went on for nearly a mile and then the trail plunged into a canebrake. The cane stood taller than Flan's head. He hesitated at the entrance to the brake. This was a fine place for an Indian ambush. He stood still, holding Meg's lead thong tightly.

Something rustled off to one side. He listened hard. Was it the wind? Or something else? The dried leaves of cane rattled. He dropped the lead line and raised his rifle. In a panic he wondered if his rifle was loaded. Supposing he'd knocked the powder from the pan? He snatched off the pan covering with trembling fingers and looked inside. With relief he saw the sprinkling of black powder in the pan.

But the thing in the cane was coming closer. Flan stepped back behind Meg. Something was definitely coming out of the brake, but he didn't think it could be Indians. It must be a bear or a catamount.

There was a gleam among the stalks of cane, and a little black and white creature strolled out onto the trace. A skunk!

A skunk! Flan grinned and watched the little animal waddling back into the cane. He turned to the horses. "I reckon you knew all along it wasn't an Injun, didn't you?" he asked Meg softly as he picked up the line. Horses could tell when Indians were close. He was daft to be so scared. He'd never get to the Lick if he was going to stop and turn over every stone, looking for a redskin.

He walked along more briskly now. The sun was shining and every step brought him closer to home. He thought back to the day when he'd stood on the bank of the Holston River with Uncle Henry and waited for Chapman Green. He wondered what Uncle Henry would think to see him now, traveling this wild country alone, taking the powder to James Robertson.

Things were different now though. He could load a gun and shoot it, he knew how to take care of the horses, he could walk a long way without getting tired. He reckoned he'd learned a heap about the woods.

He'd made a heap of friends too. There was Mr. Rhea. The trader had shown him a power of strange things along the Wilderness Trail. Flan grinned. All his life he would remember Mr. Rhea and how the trader always expected things to get worse instead of better. Flan hoped he wouldn't ever be that way.

There were the Cordells too. Mr. and Mrs. Cordell had been good to him and he'd liked Wiley, but Nancy was the one who stuck in his mind because she was unhandy like him.

He wished he could be like Nancy in other ways. It didn't seem to worry her much if she did things the wrong way. She was easy-going as a gadfly.

He thought a minute. Actually, though she couldn't do any of the things she was supposed to, she was kind of like Mr. Green, who could do so many things so well. Nancy and Mr. Green didn't fret much. They did what came along the best they knew how, and if it turned out right that was good. If it turned out wrong, well, a body couldn't do more than try.

A body couldn't do more than try. It was funny he'd got to be ten years old and not learned that. If he'd only tried he might have been pretty good at shooting and chopping by now, instead of only beginning to learn. He ought to have gone on and tried when his brothers teased him about his awkwardness.

Chapman Green had been the best friend he'd ever had, he reckoned. It wasn't just that the Long Hunter had taught him to shoot. It was because Mr. Green had always expected him to *try* to do what had to be done. Just as now he expected Flan to get this powder to the Lick. Flan, who had slowed almost to a stop as he thought over these things, gave Meg a sudden jerk and speeded up.

They went along at a good pace. A flock of passenger pigeons whirred overhead. Away off through the trees Flan could see the gleam of beech leaves and he knew the birds were headed there to feast on the nuts. He wished he had a few nuts himself. He took a handful of jerked meat from his shirt and ate it.

He stopped at a spring and let the horses drink. He sniffed the sweet smell of wet earth and watched the minnows go dashing away from the horses' mouths. "Come on, Meg, you and Brownie can eat soon if you get a move on."

He walked on and on, and the sun was high in the sky. It seemed to Flan that he ought to be getting near the French Salt Lick. He kept looking around for cleared fields or a cabin. He began to go faster, tugging at the horses who kept stopping to pull at whatever greenery they could find. He'd never known leading horses to be so hard.

The rifle got heavier with every step he took. He had to keep shifting it from hand to hand, and every time he had to swap the lead rope too. Finally he stopped.

"Maybe I'm lost," he whispered to Meg.

"Maybe we took a wrong turn somewhere." The path hadn't been worn down like the Wilderness Trail and in places it was so faint he'd had trouble following it.

The forest was so quiet he could almost feel the silence. Behind him an acorn rattled down from an oak tree. A way, way off a bird called and then it was quieter than ever.

Flan was frightened. It wasn't Indians he was afraid of now, or bears, or catamounts. It was the aloneness and the silence. He stood there among the great bare trees and cold fear crept over him until he almost turned and ran.

But Meg suddenly whinnied softly and pushed her nose into his neck. He put out his hand and caught the mare's mane.

"We'll go on a little further," he told Meg. "We still got daylight for a spell anyway."

They started off down the trace again. Flan talked to the horses to keep himself company, and then off through the trees he saw a house.

"Come along!" he shouted joyfully. "It's a blockhouse! It's the French Salt Lick for sure!"

He pulled at the lead line. "Maybe my folks are there," he said excitedly. "Maybe James Robertson will be there."

As he got nearer the house, it worried him a little that there was no sign of life, no smoke from the chimney, nobody stirring in the clearing around the house.

"Hey," he shouted from the edge of the trees. "Be this the French Salt Lick?"

There was no answer. The forest was more silent than ever. Slowly Flan made his way to the front of the building. He noticed uneasily that the door was partly open. He yelled again, but again no one answered.

Cautiously he stepped up to the door and pushed at it. The door creaked back on its wooden hinges. Through the dim light inside he made out a puncheon table and beyond it in the corner a wooden bedframe. In the fireplace were the ashes of an old fire and a smashed piggin lay on the hearth.

He stood staring into the deserted room. What had happened? Why had everybody left this

place? Were his folks all gone? Had Indians wiped out the settlement at the French Lick?

Tears of weariness stood in his eyes. Something scuttered across the floor of the second story and he turned hastily away. He was lost and worse than lost. His folks were all gone, dead, killed, captured.

He stood forlornly in the clearing wondering whether to turn back. Mr. Green was likely dead by this time. He stopped, thinking that he sounded for all the world like Mr. Rhea.

What a ninny he was! Nobody had been killed here, there weren't any graves or bodies or skeletons. The Indians hadn't captured the people. Indians never left a place standing if they could burn it. These folks had taken their pots and quilts and rifles and gone somewhere else, likely to a bigger fort. All he had to do was look for the trail and he'd get to it.

But he'd have to hurry. He'd wasted enough time already, mooning around and figuring he was lost and his folks were dead. He found the trace beyond a spring and started out at a fast clip, and this time he didn't tarry for anything. He kept going and he'd not walked more than an hour when he came to a field with a few dry stalks of corn still standing in it. He cried out for joy.

At last he saw the log blockhouse itself. It was bigger than the deserted one he'd left behind. Smoke drifted from the chimney and several horses stood tied close to the door. Two dogs came baying out to greet him and there was a scurry in the house as the door and a window shutter slammed.

Flan yelled. "Hey! Be this James Robertson's Station?"

The window opened a crack. "Nay. This is Mansker's Blockhouse. James Robertson's is twelve miles further on." There was a moment's astonished silence. "Be ye alone, lad?"

"I got two horses with me," answered Flan. By this time he had almost forgotten that Meg and Brownie weren't human beings.

"It's a lad, a mite of a boy," came a voice from

198

inside. "He's got two horses and it looks like he's got powder with him."

The door swung open and two men stepped out.

"Who are you?" the older man asked. "Where do you come from? What you got in them casks?"

Flan was a little taken aback. He'd expected a friendlier greeting than this.

"My name's Flanders Taylor. I . . . I got something for James Robertson. I'm a-looking for him and for my folks."

"Well, if it's powder you got for Jim Robertson, you ain't a minute too soon. Young feller just got here a few minutes ago to borrow some. They need powder bad down at the Bluffs. That's Robertson's Station." The man looked at Flan a minute and stroked his brown beard. "But this ain't a trick, is it? How come a boy like you bringing powder over this trail alone? A hunter named Green was who we reckoned to bring it."

In spite of all he could do tears came up in

Flan's eyes again. "It ain't no trick," he blurted out furiously. "I come from the Holston with Chapman Green. He got sick back up the trail a piece and stayed behind in a hollow sycamore, and I come on alone to try to get help for him . . ." He broke off, staring past the men at someone who stood in the doorway.

"Hank!" he said at last.

"Flan! In the nation what are you doing here? You never brung the powder alone? What ever are you doing here? What . . . how . . . you . . .?"

Flan ran and caught his oldest brother by the arm. "Tell 'em who I am," he pleaded. "Tell 'em it ain't no trick. I brung the powder all day by myself, and Mr. Green's got the ague bad and we got to go back for him!"

Hank Taylor put his arm around his brother's shoulders. "He's Flanders Taylor all right, Mr. Miles," he told the brown bearded man. "And if that's the powder Chapman Green was fetching, it's what Jim Robertson wants."

Mr. Miles laughed. "Well, lad, you've found

your folks, looks like. Taylor, you get two, three others to go back with you and you best get gone as quick as you can."

"Aye," answered Hank. "I don't want to be out after dark if I can help it. Come along, Flan, you can ride behind me on my horse to the Bluffs."

Flan held back. Hank looked at him in surprise and the younger boy shook his head. "I can't go," he said in a low voice. "I got to go back for Chapman Green."

Hank opened his mouth in astonishment, but Mr. Miles put in, "That's true. If'n we aim to find Green afore night, the boy'll have to go with us right now. There's a horse he can have, and Johnson and I will go with him."

"But how'll he get to the Bluffs?" asked Hank.

"Oh, we'll get him there," said a woman who had come out of the house. "He'll be safer here anyhow, with Indians behind every bush and tree around the Bluffs. Tell his mammy we'll take good care of him." She gave Flan a friendly smile and ruffled his hair.

"Tell Mam I'll stay till Mr. Green's well, and then I'll come with him," Flan spoke up. "I couldn't leave till I knowed he was safe. He's the best man in the world, Hank . . ."

"You'd best be off," said Mr. Miles to Hank. "It's getting late."

Flan stood while Hank and the others transferred the powder to fresh horses and rode off. He looked after them for a little while. Soon Hank would be home with Mam and Pap and Rosedel. He turned back to the blockhouse and Mr. Miles called him to come get on the horse.

A week later Mr. Green was over his ague. The Indians had given up their attack on the fort at the Bluffs and gone. Flan and the Long Hunter had ridden to the Bluffs to leave Meg and Brownie with their owner, James Robertson. And Robertson had directed them to the Taylors' cabin four miles beyond his station.

"Well," said Chapman Green to Flan as they

stood on the edge of a clearing, "I reckon you're home at last."

Flan didn't answer. He just stood gazing at the cabin. It was a bigger and better log cabin than the one they had had on the Holston—two rooms and a window in each room.

He began to walk slowly toward it. The door was open and he could see into the room. Someone was in there, moving around the fireplace. Maybe it was his mam. Suddenly he couldn't wait another moment. He began to run. A dog came barking around the corner of the house and then began to leap about him with delight.

Somebody came to the door.

"Mam! Oh, Mam!" Flan cried.

He hadn't meant to act like this, like a little boy, hugging his mammy's neck. He'd wanted to act like a man grown, and come walking in with his rifle and say gruffly, "Hello, Mam."

Rosedel came down from the loft, Hank came running from back of the cabin and went to holler for the other boys down in the field.

"Your pap's out hunting," said Mam, hugging him again. "He'll be sorry he wasn't here when you come in, but he'll be happy to see you. We been worrying about you."

His brothers came in with Chapman Green. They were so big and loud, for a minute Flan felt almost the way he used to back on the Holston. But then he saw Chapman Green, looking half his natural size among these tall sturdy black-haired young men. And Flan remembered Mr. Green running through the trees the night of the Indian fighting, looking like a man who could whip a whole Indian nation.

"It's true what Mr. Green said," he told himself, almost surprised. "It ain't size that counts. I can shoot as good as any of them." And he felt better.

"How do, Mr. Green," said Mam politely. "I hope you're over your fever."

"I'm too tough to kill, I reckon," answered the Long Hunter.

"Flan's got a rifle," yelled Alec. Alec was fifteen, the youngest of Flan's three brothers.

"What you aim to do with it, chop weeds, young 'un?"

"Give the boy time and he'll show you what he can do with it," put in Mr. Green quickly. "He's a fine shot and a brave lad. We come through a heap of bad times getting here, and more than once we'd of been bad off without him."

The brothers looked at him disbelievingly. Then they looked at Flan and shook their heads.

"He's growed," said Mam. "His shirt's most out at the seams. And his britches are short on him."

"Where'd you get the rifle?" asked Tom.

"Off an Injun I shot," answered Flan defiantly.

Tom laughed and then nudged Alec. They looked at each other and roared with laughter.

Chapman Green looked around at the three big black-haired brothers and suddenly he seemed a little angry.

"It's true," he said loudly. "He shot an Injun and saved a feller's life. And that ain't all the boy done. He saved my horses from fire at the risk of his own neck."

And then he was talking and talking and talking, telling all that Flan had done on the journey. Flan's family listened in awed silence, and sometimes Flan felt like he ought to speak up and say that he really hadn't been so brave, all the time he'd been scared to death inside, that he would never have been able to do it if Chapman Green hadn't been there expecting him to do it.

"And he come the last day of the journey all alone, to bring the powder that likely saved your skins," Chapman Green finished.

"That's so," Hank nodded. "The Chickamaugas would have scalped us sure last week if'n we hadn't had that powder."

The brothers looked solemnly at Flan. Finally Tom spoke. "I got two nice deerskins. I aimed to trade 'em, but Mam can have 'em to make you some new clothes, Flan."

"This here's my old shot pouch." Alec held

it out to his young brother. "I got a new one, so you can have this."

"Next week I'll let you ride with me over to the Bluffs and get a bullet mold," offered Hank.

"Now they're sorry they teased you, Flan," Rosedel said.

"Well," said Mam with a smile. "I made you a dried apple cobbler. It's the last of the apples I brung with us, but I didn't wait to find out you was a hero before I made it."

Flan smiled at her. "I got something for you, Mam," he said, reaching in his shirt. He drew out the wing of the goose and an ear of the deer he'd shot. "I shot them myself," he told the others.

He laid the stalactite Mr. Rhea had given him on the puncheon table. "What in the nation is that?" asked Tom.

"It's the tail of a cave rat," answered Flan soberly. "The varmints wait till you're sleeping in a cave and then they stab you with their tails."

The boys laughed and Mr. Green said approvingly, "You'll make a Long Hunter yet."

Now Flan took out the little cloth-wrapped package. He unrolled it and laid it proudly beside the other things. Everybody leaned forward to look and Mam gave a gasp.

"A silver spoon!" she breathed.

"I got it for you," Flan told her. "For saving the trader's life."

"You see, ma'am, a feller don't have to be a lawyer to get silver spoons," Mr. Green said. "You can find most anything you want out in the woods if you just know how."

"Oh, it's pretty as a red bird," exclaimed Rosedel, turning the spoon over gently.

Flan opened his mouth to speak, but he didn't know exactly how to say what he wanted to tell his mother. He wanted her to know he'd learned on the journey that it didn't matter whether a boy grew up to be a lawyer or a Long Hunter. What mattered was knowing that you could do what you had to do. What mattered was knowing you could make a few mistakes and still win if you did your best.

Mam picked up the spoon and looked at it.

"It's a fine pretty spoon," she said. "I'm proud of it." She laid the spoon down suddenly and put her arm around Flan's shoulders. "But I got no real need of silver spoons. I already got the best thing in the world. A woman with *four* fine big sons don't need nothing else."